To Mike,

ORSON
THE
GREAT

Very best wishes !

Colm McElwain

ORSON
THE
GREAT

COLM MCELWAIN

ORSON THE GREAT

Cover artwork by: germancreative on Fiverr

Proofreading service: www.abcproofreading.co.uk

ISBN-13: 978-1-3999-4569-1

Also by Colm McElwain

JAMES CLYDE AND THE DIAMONDS OF ORCHESTRA

Book One in the James Clyde series.

JAMES CLYDE AND THE TOMB OF SALVATION

Book Two in the James Clyde series.

Both books in the James Clyde series are available to purchase online through Amazon.

CHAPTER ONE

The Mystery Box

Albert Matthews walked along the crowded London street. He was around sixty years of age and was dressed formally, as if he'd just left a dinner party. Not unlike a waiter at such an event, he was attired in a black tuxedo, bow tie and a pair of white gloves.

Despite having no apparent limp or mobility issue, he walked with the aid of a distinctive black cane that had a silver skull at its top. All of a sudden, he stopped and planted his cane into the snow. He squinted his eyes before putting on his glasses.

His heart sank. Just as he had suspected.

Up ahead, at the end of the pedestrian street, an ominous black Rolls-Royce was parked with its headlights on and its engine revving. Inhaling the cold air, he kept on the move.

He crossed a busy courtyard, the public buildings on either side casting foreboding shadows over the snowy ground upon which he walked.

There were many shops, restaurants and wine bars along this way, all lit up for Christmas, and although the night was exceptionally cold, people were mingling outside.

Out of the corner of his eye, he saw the Rolls-Royce pull up at the top of the street, its headlights shining on him.

Matthews gulped. Wherever he went, the car went, too.

A moment later, the driver turned off the headlights and Matthews could see the shadowy form of the man behind the darkened window. It was definitely him. There he sat, emotionless, his hands on the steering wheel.

Matthews shook his head, a pained expression etched on his face. The man from whom he was running had contacts within the Society of Magicians that far exceeded his own.

This game of cat and mouse had to stop. His safety was compromised and he could only elude this man for so long. Stepping up onto a frosty pavement, he stumbled and bumped his way past a group of sightseers.

He had a nervous disposition at the best of times and had only volunteered for this role out of a sense of loyalty to his lifelong friend. What he didn't count on was being hunted across the city by a psychopath and his fanatical band of loyal supporters. It had to stop!

He was a magician and a part-time one at that, specialising in street performance and children's birthday parties. It was his hobby. Nothing more. He didn't deserve to be caught up in any of this.

Mixing furtively amongst the throngs of people, he stopped every so often and peered around. There was no black car following him now. None that he could see, at least.

He walked on, reminding himself that not only was he dealing with arguably the greatest magician of all time, but also the most feared.

Mercifully, his hotel was up on the left. He had a decision to make. He could either admit defeat and turn himself in, accepting whatever consequences might come his way. Or he could hide out for the night and ring the Grand Master from the relative safety of his room, before leaving first thing in the morning and travelling to the rendezvous point with the mystery box.

As Matthews made his way into the hotel, he took, from beneath the skull on his cane, a gold key and slipped it into his pocket. Another key of lesser importance was waiting for him at reception and, when he'd got it and wished the lady a Merry Christmas, he took the elevator up to the third floor and entered his room.

Encouraged, he locked the door hastily behind him and stood there in the moonlight, breathless. Closing one eye, he looked through the peephole of the door and saw an empty corridor. Rushing over to the phone by his bed, he lifted the receiver and dialled the Grand Master, who picked up after two rings.

'Were you followed?' asked the Grand Master.

'I can't be sure,' answered Matthews in a panicked voice. 'I think I've lost him.'

'Is the key safe?' asked the voice on the other line.

Matthews took the key from his pocket and set it down upon his bedside locker. 'It's right here.'

'Good,' said the Grand Master.

'Listen to me,' whispered Matthews nervously, 'it's only a matter of time until he finds me. A car was tailing me earlier. I never opened the mystery box, but I need to know. My friend, did you give me the—?'

'Don't leave your room,' the Grand Master ordered. 'See you in the morning.'

The phone went dead.

Alone with his thoughts, Matthews went across the room to close the curtains. He was in the process of doing so, when he stopped and cast his eyes down at the street below.

Even from three floors up, he could see the distinctive black Rolls-Royce parked far below.

It was him.

Matthews removed his gloves and his glasses and placed both items on his bedside locker. Then he lifted the key, threaded a chain through the hole and hung it around his neck.

Conflicted, he paced the room. The game was up. Surely, the Grand Master would understand that. It was time to end this petty feud.

Decision reached, Matthews walked over to the safe in his room, dialled in the combination and removed a black box. He set the box down upon his bed and breathed a sigh. Mustering up the courage, he made another phone call, relayed his room number and waited.

Not a minute later, he could hear the sound of footsteps slowly approaching outside in the corridor. There was a knock on his door, which he answered promptly. He knew better than to keep this man waiting.

In came the mysterious man he knew as Daxton. Whether Daxton was the man's real name or simply an alias, Matthews had no idea.

In fact, he'd only ever seen this man perform once on stage and had spoken to him on the phone twice. Up close, however, Daxton looked every inch the loathsome villain he was rumoured to be.

Aged in his early fifties, 'Daxton the Destroyer', the stage name by which he was known, had a neatly trimmed beard and a great head of curly black hair, the former tinted with flecks of grey, the latter dyed to conceal them.

He was dressed neatly in a black overcoat, navy trousers and a matching turtleneck. In his right hand, he carried a cane with a silver skull at its top.

An imposing figure, he stood at six feet four and was infamous among those in the magical community for his quick temper and fiery outbursts.

He had a pair of big, wild eyes and Matthews could feel them glaring at him now.

'You made the right decision,' said Daxton, lifting the mystery box triumphantly from the bed as if it were a pot of gold.

Matthews gave his intimidating visitor a deferential look. 'I just want peace. I hope this helps. Will it?'

Daxton stared back coldly. He didn't answer the question posed to him, but asked one of his own. 'Where's the key?'

Matthews loosened his bow tie and unbuttoned his shirt at the collar to reveal the key by his throat. 'It's right here.' He tried to unhook the chain, but he struggled as his hands were trembling.

Daxton, looking impatient, lifted a gloved hand and seized it, before ripping the chain from around Matthews' neck.

Daxton unlocked the mystery box and shook his head as he rummaged through the contents, which included two gimmick coins, a ruby-coloured silk cloth, a deck of cards and a magic pen. 'It's not here.'

Mathews sighed with relief. 'He didn't give it to me.'

Looking frustrated, Daxton said, 'Where is it then?'

Matthews held his hands in the air. 'Hey, look, there were two boxes. The pin could've been in either one of them.'

'Who has the second box?' asked Daxton. 'I need a name.'

Matthews poured himself a glass of wine. He had carried the mystery box with him for the best part of a month and he was relieved to be free of it.

'That's a good question,' he replied. 'I'm very pleased to say that I've no idea. Any one of our members might have the second box.'

Daxton looked incredulous. 'You're protecting someone. Why?'

Matthews frowned. 'Why do you want this title so badly? You're financially secure, surely?'

'It's not about money,' replied Daxton.

Matthews shrugged. 'Then what is it about?' he asked, swallowing a mouthful of wine.

'It's time for reform, Albert,' said Daxton. 'I want to get to the top of my profession. I want to taste glory. The title of Grand Master has alluded me for long enough. It shouldn't be inherited. The title should be earned!'

Matthews set his wineglass down upon a table. 'The Society of Magicians prides itself on being a democracy.'

'Does it really?!' snapped Daxton venomously. 'And yet, this family has led the Society of Magicians for decades. There is no excuse for nepotism in our community! I won't accept it! Neither should you!'

'We have elections every two years,' countered Matthews. 'If you don't like our Grand Master, then you should compete against him at the next conference. Let the jurors decide. Chasing a loophole won't do you any good. It makes you look scared of competition.'

Daxton walked over to Matthews and laid a hand upon his shoulder. 'My friend, you need to relax!'

It was a curious thing, but Matthews suddenly felt drowsy. Not having gone far, he tried to reach the table to steady himself; but, unable to make it that far, he had to sit down on the nearest chair.

Daxton placed his hand back on Matthews' shoulder, a little firmer this time. 'As you listen to my voice, you'll go deeper and deeper into your unconscious mind.'

Matthews' eyelids fluttered.

Daxton looked determined. 'No more lies,' he said in a soft tone of voice. 'Who has the second mystery box?'

'Orson,' muttered Matthews, struggling to keep his eyes open.

'The Destroyer' shook his head. 'And who might that be?'

'Surely you've heard of "Orson the Great"?' said Matthews.

'I'm competing against the Grand Master's son?' said Daxton in surprise. 'The young boy?'

'That's right,' said Matthews. 'Orson will soon be sworn in as our new Grand Master.'

Daxton shook his head. 'I've met him a couple of times, but he's never struck me as being special. Why choose him? He can't beat me.'

'He's a precocious talent,' retorted Matthews. 'If he lives up to his promise, then he'll be an incredible magician one day. Even better than—'

Daxton arched his eyebrows.

'Well, you,' resumed Matthews.

Daxton brooded over this comment for a moment.

'Don't underestimate him,' added Matthews. 'He *can* beat you next Christmas!'

'I'm going to count to five,' said Daxton, 'and when I reach five, you'll be fully awake and unaware of what has passed between us. One.' He began to walk towards the door. 'Two.' He found his cane. 'Three.' He opened the door. 'Four.' He looked back at Matthews. 'You really believe this boy can beat me?'

'No offence,' said Matthews, 'but if there was one person that I would put my faith in to beat you, then it would be Orson the Great.'

Daxton was taken aback. 'You're wrong and I'm going to prove it!'

'How will you prove it?' asked Matthews, coming around slowly.

Daxton stepped outside into the corridor, but turned back to close the door. 'You'll see. I've unfinished business with this so-called "Orson the Great". Five.' He closed the door behind him.

Then he was gone.

CHAPTER TWO

Christmas, 1972

Famed magician Orson Whitlock hadn't even finished his performance when his best friend Agatha, professionally working as his assistant, approached unscripted and handed him a note.

It struck him as strange, but by now he'd fallen into a train of thought and, unwilling to break his concentration, he pocketed the slip of paper in his jacket. He peered out at the full house.

The theatre was packed with people who'd travelled from far and wide to witness his jaw-dropping feats. This was the finale, not just of tonight's performance, but of the entire sold-out tour.

The travelling magic show had performed throughout Europe to widespread acclaim, mystifying audiences in cities from Vienna and Paris to Dublin and now London.

At just twelve years of age, Orson had performed before royalty, presidents, prime ministers and anyone else wishing to see the much-heralded child prodigy in action.

His shows were renowned for their large-scale production values and amazing spectacles, with elaborate lighting displays and death-defying acts of escapism commonplace.

Card tricks, mentalism, close-up magic, levitations and hypnosis were cornerstones of Orson's performance, and yet audience interaction and participation were also key elements of his routine.

He sometimes shared the stage with a sixty-piece symphony orchestra and, while this undoubtedly enhanced the show, even the pompous conductor Ralph Neumann would concede, and often did, that the queues in the square before the show were for one man only – 'Orson the Great'.

'Why, thank you,' said Orson, wrapping the gold-plated glass locket, supplied by the chosen volunteer Katherine Hall, in a white towel. 'An exquisite piece. Expensive, I'm sure?'

The young woman, who was dressed in her finest clothes, gave a concerned nod and frowned. 'The locket belonged to my late grandmother and it's very dear to my heart. It's an heirloom and has been in our family for generations. Our family name is engraved on it.'

'How lovely,' said Orson.

Katherine Hall made a face. 'Maybe this is a mistake,' she protested. 'Take my watch instead!'

Orson patted the towel. 'No, no, the locket will do just fine.'

Katherine Hall looked regretful. 'But my watch doesn't have any sentimental value. Honestly, just take my watch—'

'You have no need to worry,' Orson assured her, grabbing her wrist. 'I'll take good care of your locket.'

'You do seem like a nice kid,' said the woman, looking reassured.

'Thank you,' replied Orson. 'I also happen to have a terrific professional indemnity insurance policy.'

The volunteer, whose eyes were on the towel in Orson's hands, laughed nervously. 'Please tell me you're joking!'

Orson shook his head. 'No, Miss. Insurance is essential in my line of work.'

Right on schedule, the special effects team released the theatrical fog onto the stage, shrouding both magician and participant in mystery and danger. At the same time, the orchestra ramped up the dramatic music to amplify the tension.

The cameras zoomed in closer, affording spectators in the gallery and those craning their necks in the corner seats a clearer image of the action unfolding on the giant screen behind the stage.

Orson led the woman over to the edge of the stage and stopped when he reached a wooden table, upon which lay a sledgehammer.

'Now, Katherine,' he said, taking up the sledgehammer, 'will you please confirm to our lovely audience that we've never met before.'

Katherine Hall never diverted her eyes from the sledgehammer in the young magician's hand. 'I've never spoken to you before in my life,' she replied.

'Perfect!' said Orson, grinning out at the audience as he laid the towel with the enclosed locket down upon the table. 'Just the answer we rehearsed backstage.'

The audience in the packed theatre laughed, then gasped when Orson the Great smashed the towel five times with the sledgehammer. Then a sixth for good measure.

With each audible smash, the women in the front two rows jumped, their hands instinctively reaching for their necklaces, fearing that a request for another item of considerable worth was imminent from the young magician.

Katherine Hall recoiled in horror and clasped a hand to her mouth. She had no words.

Orson produced a silver-plated watch from his tux pocket and showed it to Katherine. 'A watch like any other?'

Katherine Hall still had no words.

Orson smiled mischievously. 'What if I told you that the possessor of this watch can go back in time and alter events. Would you believe me?'

'I want to believe you, yes!' cried Katherine Hall, her eyes fixed on the battered towel.

Orson resumed. 'In order to achieve these amazing feats, I need the audience to believe that the impossible is truly possible.' He wound his pocket watch back by one minute and then set it down upon the table. Next, he lifted the towel and unfolded it slowly. The locket, smashed or otherwise, was no longer inside.

Before Katherine Hall could utter a word, she discovered her locket back around her neck. The engraving of the family name 'Hall' marked it out as uniquely hers.

'How did you do that?' exclaimed the young woman.

'Oh, I almost forgot,' said Orson, reaching into his jacket pocket and removing a beautiful Rolex wristwatch. 'I believe you told me to take your watch as well?!'

Katherine Hall groped for a watch that was no longer on her wrist. 'You took my watch too?!' she cried. 'How'd you get that?'

'Magic,' said Orson. He lit a slip of paper in his hand with a match and, after a quick flash, it transformed into a single red rose. He handed it to the volunteer and thanked her kindly for being a good sport.

The spellbound audience rose to their feet and began to applaud.

Soaking up the adulation, Orson bowed his head and waved his hands out triumphantly. 'Thank you!' he exclaimed. 'Thank you all for coming!'

With the spotlight following his every move, he escorted a delighted Katherine Hall over to the stairs and watched her return to the audience with a beaming smile upon her face.

Agatha came rushing on stage and promptly placed the magician's cape over Orson's shoulders, signalling the end of the performance.

The fog increased and, by the time Orson had placed his top hat on his head, he could barely be seen on stage.

The crowd begged for one more trick, which was heartening for Orson to hear. However, the red curtains had already begun to close and the orchestra had struck up a suitably rousing piece, drowning out the cheers.

In high spirits, Orson listened to the rapturous applause. He was at the top of his game, the youngest ever magician to sell out venues around the world.

He raised his arms out wide, waiting for the curtains to reopen. When they parted, he saw the audience in the stalls standing to applaud him. He raised his eyes. All the people in the galleries and upper boxes were on their feet, too.

'Thank you,' he mouthed. 'You're very kind. Thank you so much!'

He stole another look around the house and his attention was drawn to the front row, where something struck him as strange. Throughout the entire performance, one seat in the row had remained reserved, but unoccupied. The scene had changed. He did a double take. A large, bearded man was sitting there now.

The man in the front row was wearing a fine black suit and his gloved hands clasped a cane with a silver skull on the top of it. He just sat there, staring up at Orson intently.

Although their eyes met for just a moment, a spark of recognition presented itself between them. The colour drained from Orson's face. It couldn't be!

Orson squinted to see his great rival, but the artificial fog had roamed from the stage to the front row and 'Daxton the Destroyer' was obscured.

The curtains closed.

It was not until Orson had removed his white gloves that he remembered Agatha's note and promptly found it in his jacket pocket. He glanced around the staging area, searching for Agatha, his face expressing worry and terror in equal measure. She was nowhere to be seen.

He looked down at the gold pin on his jacket. It glinted under the stage lights, but the title it represented suddenly weighed heavily on his shoulders.

Half a dozen stagehands congratulated him on a great show, but his mind was elsewhere. He thanked them, but ran off stage, his cape billowing behind him.

When he had found a quiet area, he sat down on a step and read the note to himself in a low voice. *'Daxton has found you!'*

He got back to his feet and walked past a couple of trombone players, who were placing their instruments back into their cases. They smiled and nodded at him courteously as he went by.

The stage was already cleared and Orson could hear, on the other side of the curtains, the murmurings of the departing crowd.

Through the gap at the side of one curtain, he peeked out at the front row. A small cluster of people were trickling out of the theatre and the front row had already been vacated. Daxton had departed. Orson sighed and stood for a moment to compose himself.

Just then, Agatha raced forward, grabbed him by the hand and hurried him along the wing of the theatre.

'Are you sure it was him?' asked Orson, sounding panicked.

Agatha grimaced. 'Yeah, I am,' she said, quickening her pace. 'He's backstage!'

'What?!' cried Orson. 'He's backstage?'

'He's looking for you!' said Agatha, hurrying past a woman holding a clarinet. 'You need to get out of here and head back to the hotel right away.'

Orson didn't argue with any of this.

'I'm going straight there now, too,' said Agatha, releasing Orson's hand when they had reached the exit door. 'Daxton knows what I look like now. I'm not safe here, either.'

Orson turned around. 'I'm so sorry for getting you involved in all of this. You must hate me.'

'I do,' said Agatha with a smirk. 'With a passion!'

'Huh?' cried Orson. 'Do you hate me?'

'You kidding?' said Agatha. 'There isn't a dull moment when I'm with you. It's one adventure after another.'

Orson laughed. 'And that's a good thing, is it?' he asked.

Agatha rolled her eyes. 'Yes, that's a good thing.' She pushed Orson towards the exit door. 'Except when psychopaths like Daxton are chasing after us. Now, get out of here. Go!'

Orson half-smiled at her. Then he left.

CHAPTER THREE

The Clockmaker

The flash of camera bulbs blinded Orson when he exited the venue through the side door. Attempting to make a quick getaway was nigh on impossible, as he was detained by overzealous fans and autograph hunters, all of whom were clamouring to meet him.

Ever the professional, he didn't disappoint, signing 'Orson the Great' on posters, programmes, flyers and anything else that was handed to him.

Security, comprising of three hefty men in black suits, battled through the crowds and eventually helped Orson into his limousine, which sped off quickly, leaving his eager fans behind.

A little later, Orson's chauffeur rolled down the partition divider. He was a stout little man with a moustache. 'Good evening, Mr Whitlock. How was the show?'

'Went very well, thank you,' replied Orson, glancing suspiciously out his side window at a passing car.

'Didn't make anyone disappear, I hope?' said the driver.

'I did, actually,' replied Orson with a nod, 'but I made her reappear soon afterwards.'

The driver laughed. 'If you need anything, just press the buzzer.'

'I know it sounds crazy,' said Orson, turning around and looking out the rear window at the row of cars behind them. 'But make sure you're not followed.'

The driver looked perplexed. 'Followed, Mr Whitlock? Are you expecting company?'

'I hope not!' said Orson, exchanging looks with the driver.

A few minutes later, the driver pulled into the reserved parking space just outside the hotel.

The concierge came rushing out, the boot of the car was swiftly opened and the luggage promptly wheeled into the lobby, before heading up on a lift to room five hundred and four.

Orson ascended the marble stairs, pushed through the revolving doors and walked into the luxurious lobby. There, he spotted Agatha already standing at the main reception, taking care of the reservation.

Orson stood within earshot, observing her.

'How did the show go?' asked the receptionist, Ms Ford, when Agatha had covered the cost of the stay in advance.

'It was amazing,' said Agatha. 'Best crowd of the entire tour.'

'Well, I'd a feeling,' said Ms Ford. 'We had journalists in earlier today enquiring if Mr Whitlock was staying here. Then we'd autograph hunters of all ages, with magic wands and top hats, queuing outside the doors. In my thirty-five years working here, I've never seen the like of it.'

All this time, Orson paced up and down the spacious lobby nervously.

'The superstar himself,' said Ms Ford, nodding at Orson.

When the revolving doors rotated and a man with a black cane ambled in, Orson turned in terror. The man in question didn't look anything like

'Daxton the Destroyer', but the mere sound of a cane clacking on the tiles was enough to send Orson into a panic. He waved his hands in the air, urging Agatha to speed things up a bit.

'Is he all right?' asked Ms Ford, gazing at Orson in bewilderment. 'Is he always this nervous after a show?'

'Sometimes,' replied Agatha.

Ms Ford smiled. 'Wait until he sees his room,' she said proudly. 'That should put his mind at ease. He's in the presidential suite. President Nixon and the first lady stayed in the very same room in 1969. Simply glorious.'

'Oh, how lovely,' exclaimed Agatha.

Ms Ford started to laugh uproariously. 'You'll have to make do with a single room on the second floor. Much smaller room, but it's not too shabby, I can assure you.'

Agatha looked around the opulent lobby. 'I'm sure I'll survive.'

From behind the reception desk, Ms Ford lifted a box full to the brim with fan mail and placed it down on the desk with a thud. 'I presume you take this. Careful, it's very heavy.'

'Thanks for all your help,' said Agatha, wrestling the box down from the desk.

'Goodnight, Ms Anderson,' said the receptionist with a smile.

Agatha carried the box with both hands and crossed the lobby towards the elevator.

Orson joined her. 'D'you need a hand with that?'

'I'm fine,' said Agatha, delighted to finally drop the box of fan mail down on the floor.

Orson pushed the golden button on the wall to summon the elevator.

'Are you still worried about Daxton?' asked Agatha.

'Worried is too strong a word,' said Orson uneasily. 'Concerned maybe.'

Agatha lowered her glasses and smiled at him. 'Same thing. Don't be worried or concerned.'

'Yeah, well, you seemed worried back at the theatre, too,' Orson told her.

Agatha shrugged. 'A little, maybe,' she admitted. 'He's toying with you. That's all it is. He's trying to get in your head before tomorrow's contest. Don't let him!'

The elevator doors opened and five people walked out.

When the last person had left, Agatha lifted the box of fan mail and stepped into the cabin of the elevator.

'How did he find me?' said Orson hurriedly, following her in.

Agatha burst out laughing. 'How did he find you?'

Orson gave a quick nod.

Agatha groaned. 'Are you being modest?'

'Nope,' said Orson, noticing a woman in the foyer rushing towards the elevator. He made a gesture towards her to see if she wanted the elevator doors held open, but she shook her head and walked instead towards the restaurant.

The elevator doors closed.

'You're one of the most famous magicians in the world,' said Agatha. 'Of course he was going to find you! No need to panic, though. London is a big place. He doesn't know what hotel you're staying in, let alone what room. Push level two, will you?'

Orson raised his thumb and pushed the number two on the button selection.

'Besides, he's running out of time,' said Agatha. 'He's getting desperate.'

'That's what scares me,' said Orson cautiously. 'What time is the taxi tomorrow?'

Agatha smiled. 'Half past eleven.'

'Okay, good,' replied Orson. 'The sooner we get to the venue tomorrow, the better.'

'We'll talk about it in the morning,' said Agatha. She handed Orson his room key.

'What floor am I on?' asked Orson.

Agatha pushed the number five button with her elbow. 'The fifth,' she replied.

The elevator stopped with a ping on the second floor.

Agatha got out and smiled. 'Lay low. Stay in your room and you'll be fine.'

Orson pointed down at the box of fan mail. 'Am I taking this?'

'They're your fans,' said Agatha, laughing.

Having recovered his composure, Orson shook his head and smiled. 'And you're my assistant.'

'Don't forget to lock your door,' said Agatha.

Orson laughed. 'I thought you said I was safe here.'

The doors of the elevator began to close.

'Just in case!' replied Agatha with a shrug. 'See you in the restaurant for breakfast at nine o'clock tomorrow. Sleep tight.'

Orson took a deep breath and listened as the elevator rumbled upwards. The elevator ascended three more flights and, when it stopped and the doors parted, he lifted the box and began the short walk to his room.

On his way, he met a young woman walking towards the elevator.

'Great show tonight,' she said, her face beaming. 'I took my eight-year-old daughter. We absolutely loved it!'

Switching into character mode immediately, Orson smiled warmly and delivered his rote response with typical charisma and charm.

The woman looked delighted as she entered the elevator.

Room five hundred and four was the first door along the corridor when Orson emerged from the elevator. He unlocked the door, walked inside and set the box of fan mail down on the floor. Switching on a lamp, he wandered around. What a room it was!

There were four different quarters: each one overwhelming with its luxury and connected by sliding white doors. Orson did a quick tour.

The living room was adorned with four couches, three large chandeliers and two Christmas trees in opposite corners.

In the bedroom were twenty-seven cushions, six wardrobes, a remote-controlled television and a bed valued at thirty thousand pounds.

The lavish bathroom boasted a huge shower, a jacuzzi tub, an en suite sauna – and, thank goodness for that, for Orson didn't see it at first amongst all the other elegance, a toilet.

He carried on.

The room in which he now stood had another remote-controlled television, a dining table set for eight, and two fridges stocked with food. Other nice touches included cabinets full of chocolate treats and nibbles. He was spoilt for choice.

Orson carefully removed his cape and hung it up. Then he emptied all his pockets. He laid on the table before him a ruby-red silk cloth, two fake thumb tips made of plastic, four slips of flash paper, three sponge balls, one gimmick coin, a bent spoon and a black fountain pen with an elastic string attached to its lid. Lastly, out came the slip of paper on which was written, '*Daxton has found you!*'

Although fears had undoubtedly crept into his psyche, Orson felt more resolute since finding sanctuary in his room. He ripped the slip of paper into pieces and threw each one in the bin. He would deal with things in the morning.

With the exception of Daxton's surprise appearance in the audience, the show tonight had actually been a fitting end to a hugely successful tour.

Orson went over to the window and gazed out.

It was only two days until Christmas and, across from his hotel, there was a festive market lined with decorated stalls selling everything from mulled wine and punch to gingerbread biscuits, Spanish paella and French crêpes.

Even at this hour, the street was lively and the scent of whatever Christmas dishes were cooking far below wafted into his room.

Never one to eat before a show, Orson was now famished. In keeping with his usual post-performance ritual, he phoned down for room service and very soon the twenty-four-hour butler assigned to his room was knocking on his door.

He sat and ate by the window, enjoying the sights and joys of the season – the bustling London street had been transformed into a Christmas wonderland.

Through the snow, he could see Westminster Bridge twinkling with Christmas lights and the shadowy forms of the many people walking across it.

When the butler returned half an hour later to collect the dishes, Orson felt like himself again.

'You didn't seem to enjoy that?' said the butler, looking at the spotless plate.

Orson laughed. Then he slurped the last few drops of his pint of milk through a straw.

'Dessert, Mr Whitlock?' asked the butler, whipping a red cloth from the top of a trolley, as if he were a fellow magician, to reveal a selection of sweet treats.

Orson's eyes lit up. After much consideration, he selected the crème brûlée with shortbread over the lemon meringue pie, and added a dollop of whipped cream from a jug he'd discovered on the second tier of the trolley.

'Ah, wonderful choice,' said the butler. 'I'd some earlier. Delicious.' The butler walked over to the open window and closed it slightly. 'Will there be anything else, sir?'

'No thanks,' replied Orson, eating his dessert in forkfuls.

About to leave, the butler paused. 'I've a daughter around your age. She's a massive fan.' From his pocket, he removed a small notepad that was usually used for taking orders. 'She adores you and Elvis Presley. I don't know in what order. The Beatles as well, before they split up.'

Orson smiled. 'I'm in good company.'

'Any chance of an—?'

Orson raised his eyebrows. 'Autograph?'

'Would you mind?' asked the butler.

Orson laid his fork down upon the table. 'Not at all. What's her name?'

'Lucy. Write something funny, too, would you?'

Orson took a pen from his jacket pocket and scribbled on the notepad.

The butler, Lucy's father, smiled when he took the notepad back. 'To Lucy, sorry I'm not Elvis. Best wishes, Orson Whitlock. She's going to love this. It'll make her Christmas. Thank you.'

Suddenly, a great commotion erupted down in the street below.

Orson hurried over to the window, pressed his nose against the pane of glass and peered down. A black Rolls-Royce had skidded in the snow and had almost collided with another car in a race to get the last parking space outside the hotel.

'A brand new 1972 Rolls-Royce,' said the butler, joining Orson by the window.

The owner of the other car, which was a Ford Cortina, was standing out in the snow, gesturing angrily at the occupant of the Rolls-Royce, who, unwilling to engage, remained hidden inside his blacked-out vehicle.

'Can I ask you a question, Mr Whitlock?' said the butler, shaking his head at the unpleasant spectacle below.

Orson nodded. 'Of course you can.'

'How'd you get so good at magic?' enquired the butler.

Orson smiled. 'My father.'

'Your father?' said the butler in surprise. 'I read somewhere that your father was a horologist. A clockmaker!'

Orson had a twinkle in his eye. 'Oh, he was a lot more than just a clockmaker!'

CHAPTER FOUR

The Uninvited Visitor

Orson awoke with a start on the couch. The room was flashing and he heard a window smash. He scratched his head. What was going on? The shrieks of panicked voices filled the air. A dog was barking.

Then all hell broke loose. A series of gunshots rang out, causing people to scream at one another in desperation. Doors flung open, then slammed shut; more windows were smashed, cars tyres squealed and ambulance sirens blared.

Rubbing his eyes, he stared at the action unfolding in the movie for a moment, before getting up and turning off the television. For all the luxuries that adorned his suite, he couldn't see a clock of any description.

It was still very dark and, as tended to happen after a performance, he'd fallen asleep in his clothes. He got up and went into the next compartment via the connecting doors, hunting for a clock.

If it was time to get up, he'd take a shower, get dressed and go downstairs for breakfast. Otherwise, he'd simply get changed into his pyjamas and go back to bed.

Illuminated in the golden lights of the two Christmas trees, Orson made his way around the living room and saw the only clock in the room, which stated it was one forty-five. The time was confirmed not a moment later by the sound of nearby Big Ben chiming for the quarter hour.

The famous clock tower landmark was visible from his room and yet he'd gone searching for a clock! He felt a little foolish, but attributed this misstep down to tiredness.

He was about to return to bed and had loosened the top button of his shirt, when he tripped over the box of fan mail, scattering letters and cards across the carpet.

Gathering them up, he threw a bunch of letters back into the box. However, even in the dim moonlight, one that remained on the floor caught his eye. He looked anxiously at it for a moment, then picked it up. It was a white envelope with a black-coloured skull embossed on it.

Rushing over to the window, Orson ripped open the envelope and read the handwriting under the moonlight. *'I said I'd find you. Daxton.'*

No sooner had he finished reading the note, than his eyes were drawn to the black Rolls-Royce parked below. It was the only car still there.

Just then, the elevator outside his room pinged. Scampering across his room, Orson held one eye to the peephole; however, although the door to the elevator was open, he couldn't see anybody in the corridor. Shaking his head, he went back to the window and beheld a strange sight below.

The Rolls-Royce was gone and in its place was the imprint of a skull in the snow. Orson suddenly felt like he was the participant in somebody's else's magic show.

Trying to suppress his rising fear, he sat down on the couch, but stood back up immediately when he observed a shadow forming underneath the door. Holding his breath, he waited for the person on the other side of the door to knock, or perhaps say something.

A sudden scream from outside made him look towards the window. What was that? He was about to cross his room to investigate, when the handle of his door started to turn. His heart began to race. Had he locked the door?

Glued to the spot, Orson watched on in terror, but the door stood firm, despite the best efforts of the person on the other side. Repeatedly, the uninvited visitor turned the door handle, but couldn't get in.

Next moment, the shadow beneath the door vanished.

Orson exhaled.

Perhaps it had simply been a late-night reveller who'd mistakenly gone to the wrong room. This thought was still processing in his mind, when an eerie sensation came over him.

Orson felt a sudden chill blast of air, as if another door had been opened. A secret one, perhaps. A feeling of dread swept over him, and he became conscious of another presence in his room.

The sound of swift footsteps caused him to look wildly around. Out of the shadows, a lurking figure dressed in black stole into his view.

Orson made a run for the door, and was quite close to it, when a gloved hand covered his mouth from behind and he was wrenched backwards.

In desperation, Orson tried to scream, but his attempts were muffled, and who was going to hear him, anyway?

Gasping for breath, his imagination tried to conjure an explanation for the presence of an intruder in his room, and his mind settled on the one that he intuitively knew to be true.

Daxton has found me!

CHAPTER FIVE

How It All Began

It was two years earlier, at the tender age of ten, when Orson fell deeply and passionately in love with magic. It was in the early hours of Christmas Eve when he was awakened by his father.

'Merry Christmas, Orson,' said his dad excitedly.

Orson rubbed his eyes and sat up in bed. 'Merry Christmas, Dad,' he replied sleepily.

'Follow me, and be quiet,' whispered Martin Whitlock. 'Don't wake your mother.'

Orson peered up at the diverse collection of wonderful-looking clocks adorning his bedroom walls, each one playing a different melody whenever they struck the hour.

Most solely told the time, but there were several hand-crafted cuckoo clocks that took his father well over a year to design and make.

There was a clock with twelve playing cards representing each hour, the long and short hands shaped like magic wands; the former was pointing to the ten of hearts, the latter to the four of diamonds.

His eyes found his favourite clock: on the chime, a magician in a top hat would burst out and make a rabbit disappear with his wand, before reversing to the door through which he'd appeared.

However, simple or lavish, big or small, each clock told the same time: it was ten minutes to four.

Orson threw off his blankets. Then he found his slippers underneath the radiator and put on his bed robe as quickly as he could.

'Remember to be quiet,' said Orson's dad, holding a finger to his lips.

Before Orson had a chance to ask what was going on, he was being led out the door, past his father's workshop and into the living room where, in an adjoining conservatory, the Christmas tree stood in all its majestic glory.

Orson gazed up at the Star of Bethlehem, then back at his dad for some answers.

His dad was pointing a finger down at the presents.

Falling to his knees, Orson looked at the presents underneath the tree, then up at his dad in a haze of tiredness and puzzlement. He tried to form a sentence, but it was cut short by his father.

'I know, Orson,' he said, his eyes bright. 'I'm a day early, but I can't wait until Christmas morning. This is important.'

'What's important?' said Orson with a yawn.

Martin Whitlock pointed to a small present wrapped in gold paper and hiding underneath a pile of parcels, like a precious jewel buried beneath rubble. 'I need you to open your present!'

On his hands and knees, Orson crawled forward and nudged a few larger presents out of the way with his elbow to get to the appointed one.

'Just don't tell your mum we opened a present before Christmas Day,' said Orson's dad.

'A deck of cards?' said Orson in bewilderment, when he'd unwrapped the present. He was woken in the middle of the night for a deck of cards!

'Not just any old deck of cards, Orson,' replied his father, reading Orson's mind. 'Well, they are old, actually, but that's the point!'

It took Orson a moment to reflect on all of this. He looked up innocently at his dad.

'These cards have been passed down from generation to generation,' said Martin Whitlock. 'They were given to me by my father when I was eleven years old, and now I am passing them over to you.'

Orson shrugged. 'Why?'

'Magic is in our blood,' replied Orson's dad passionately. 'The Whitlock family name is synonymous with magic. I want you to carry on the tradition.'

'But you make clocks, Dad,' said Orson. 'You're not a magician.'

Martin Whitlock looked serious. 'Oh, I'm a lot more than just a clockmaker!' He removed the cards from their glass casing and began shuffling and cutting them confidently, like a dealer at a poker table.

Orson's eyes could hardly keep up. 'Wow, how'd you do that?' he said, awake now and looking attentively at his dad.

Orson's dad smiled. 'This is a trick I want to teach you.' He fanned the cards out, face up. 'Fifty-two cards and you can see they're all different?'

Orson's eyes inspected each card.

'Can't you, Orson?' said his dad with a smile.

Orson nodded. 'Yep, they're all different.'

Martin Whitlock did another shuffle and spread the cards out again, face down this time. 'Pick a card, any card,' he instructed.

Orson picked a card.

'You're sure?' asked his dad. 'It's a free choice. You can pick another card.'

Resisting the urge to change his mind, Orson shook his head and clasped the card close to his chest. 'I'll stick with this one.'

'You can look at it,' replied Orson's dad. 'But don't tell me what the card is.'

Orson nodded, peeked down at his card and observed that it was the six of spades.

'Now, return your chosen card back into the pack,' asked his father, spreading the cards. 'Anywhere you like.'

Orson returned his selected card back into the middle of the deck.

His dad smiled. 'Now, watch closely.' He shuffled the cards a few times to make sure that the chosen card was lost and then began to deal them face up on the carpet. 'Tell me to stop when you see your card.'

Orson looked at each card as it landed face up on the carpet. In particular, he kept his eyes peeled for the spade suits. He was about to shout 'stop' when he spotted the nine of spades, thinking that it was his card, but realised his mistake just in the nick of time.

When every single card was dealt face up on the carpet, Orson looked up at his dad.

'You never said stop,' said Martin Whitlock, laughing.

'I didn't see my card,' replied Orson.

Orson's dad frowned. 'Are you sure?'

'Yes,' answered Orson.

'What was your card?'

'The six of spades,' replied Orson, rummaging around the cards on the carpet. 'It's not there.'

'That's interesting,' said his dad, rubbing his chin. He raised a finger towards the Christmas tree. 'Do you see the brownish envelope hanging on the tree?'

Orson looked over his shoulder and saw a light-brown envelope tied to a branch of the Christmas tree by a pink ribbon. 'What's that?' he asked.

'It's a prediction.'

Orson smiled. 'A prediction?'

'What if I told you,' said Martin Whitlock, returning the smile, 'that the six of spades was now in that envelope. Wouldn't that be amazing?'

Orson laughed.

'Well, wouldn't it, Orson?' asked his dad again.

Orson looked dubious. 'Yeah! Just a bit. It would be impossible.'

Orson's dad stared back at him. 'What did we sit down to watch last summer?'

'Last summer?' said Orson, thinking back. 'Erm, Apollo 11. The moon landing.'

His father raised a finger in the air. 'Exactly, Orson. We put men on the moon! Nothing is impossible.'

Like picking an apple from a tree, Orson reached up and plucked the envelope down. 'Can I open it?'

'Watch carefully,' said Martin Whitlock, waving his hand over the envelope and clicking his fingers. 'Now you can open it.'

Orson peeled the envelope open slowly, willing it to be the six of spades. With his fingertips, he slid the card out and his heart sank. How could he break this to his dad? In the end, he didn't have to – his disappointed face told the whole story.

His dad grimaced. 'You don't look impressed?'

Orson gave a sheepish shrug and turned the card over. 'Sorry, Dad, it's the king of hearts.'

'Oh, dear,' replied his dad, looking melancholy.

Orson hugged his dad. 'Don't worry, Dad. Better luck next time. Maybe you could try another trick? An easier one.'

'What do you mean?' asked his dad in astonishment. 'I got it right.'

'But Dad—'

'You're not really looking, Orson,' admonished his father. 'You don't really want to believe in magic! And unless you want to believe, then I'm wasting my time giving you this deck of cards!'

Orson shook his head. 'But Dad, it's not the right card. I've checked—'

'There are two types of people, Orson,' cried his father passionately. 'Those who believe in magic and those who don't! You don't believe in magic!'

'I do!' said Orson.

'Then say it and mean it!' his father demanded. 'Do you believe in magic or not?'

'I believe in magic,' cried Orson.

'Then look closer, my boy. Look closer!'

Orson lifted the card to his eyes and, at first, he couldn't see anything except the king of hearts. In fact, the more he tried *not* to see the king of hearts, the more he *saw* kings and hearts. Admittedly, the king did look slightly different, but what was it?

In his hand, the king held a *something* – not a sword or a shield, but a card. Upon closer inspection, Orson realised it was, in fact – the six of spades! *The six of spades!*

Orson ran around the room, waving the king of hearts in the air. 'He's holding the six of spades! Dad, the king's holding the six of spades! You did it! Oh, do another one!'

'I was hoping you'd say that,' replied Orson's dad. 'And that's precisely why I won't! Now, back to bed.'

'Huh?' said Orson. 'Dad, you've just woken me up. I won't be able to sleep now. How did you do that? Please tell me.'

His father smiled. 'All in good time, but I want you to remember how you feel right now. This is how your audience should always feel. Never forget that.'

Orson looked up at his dad, then down at the card in his hand.

'This leads me onto my next point,' Martin Whitlock told his son. 'Always leave your audience wanting more!' He took the card off Orson and slid it back into the envelope. 'For you.' He held the envelope outward. 'See you in the morning.'

Orson took the envelope and reluctantly started off back to bed. When he got into bed a few minutes later, he sat up, turned on his bedside lamp and carefully inspected the king of hearts.

More importantly, he studied the six of spades that the king held in his hand. Orson slipped the card back into the envelope and placed it under his pillow.

One thing he knew for certain, as he drifted to sleep finally, was that his father was wrong about one thing – he *did* believe in magic!

CHAPTER SIX

Charisma

Under the guidance of his father, Orson flourished. By the time he'd turned eleven, he was proficient at cards. When most children his age were learning how to knot a tie, Orson could perform incredible magic tricks with playing cards.

Magic consumed his mind and he devoted himself to it constantly. He could think of nothing else and practised every morning, noon and night until he had perfected every trick.

There were cards found lying at the bottom of his school bag, in his pencil case, his shoes, between the cushions of the couch, and on the top shelf of the kitchen cupboard where his mum hid the chocolate.

A deck of cards never left his hand. He could create effects using challenging and difficult sleight-of-hand techniques and manipulate choices through psychological practices.

False shuffles, one-handed cuts, card palms and passes became second nature to him. When Christmas came around again, thoughts coalesced in his mind about what element of magic he would now progress onto.

So, when he was awoken early on a wintry December morning and followed his father into the living room, he expected anything from a straitjacket escape routine to a fire cage to be waiting for him under the Christmas tree.

Indeed, there were some impressively large gifts by the foot of the tree, but his father was pointing to a small, square-shaped present amongst them all.

'Another deck of cards?' asked Orson in surprise as he reached for his present.

Orson's father shook his head and smiled. 'No, Orson, even more important.'

Heart racing, Orson ripped the present open and flung the blue wrapping paper on the floor. He couldn't believe his eyes.

'A dictionary!' he cried, looking around the base of the tree for anything else that might've fallen out and was now hiding somewhere beneath the mountain of presents.

Martin Whitlock smiled. 'Merry Christmas, son!'

'Merry what?' Orson flicked through the pages with indifference. 'Oh, right, Merry Christmas to you too, Dad.' He brought the dictionary closer to his face. 'So, what's the secret?'

Orson's dad looked puzzled. 'The what?'

Orson found himself raising his voice. 'The secret, Dad! I can't see it. It's obviously a prop of some description.' He turned the dictionary upside down and shook it like a snow globe. 'Is there a secret compartment somewhere? Maybe there's a hidden key that opens a lock into a secret vault that contains—'

'I'll stop you there. It's an English dictionary.'

Orson looked back at his dad, stunned.

His father swiped the dictionary off him and waved it in the air. 'Keep this dictionary safe,' he told Orson. 'You might need it for more than just words one day.'

Orson groaned. 'But where's the magic?'

Orson's father flipped through the pages of the dictionary as if it were a deck of cards. 'The magic is right here in these pages,' he said. 'You'll get your main present on Christmas Eve. Now, say "stop" whenever you like.'

Orson rolled his eyes. 'Stop!'

Martin Whitlock ran his fingertip down the page. 'Mmm,' he mumbled. 'Let me see. So "e". Ah yes, do you know what the word "exquisite" means?'

'No, I don't,' said Orson, looking on in disbelief. 'I've a feeling you're going to tell me, though.'

'Extremely beautiful and delicate,' replied his father, pointing down at the word. 'You tell your girlfriend in school someday that her dress looks exquisite and you'll see her reaction. Words matter. Language is magic.'

'I don't have a girlfriend in school,' replied Orson indignantly. 'I think you already know that, though.'

'You asked me, Orson,' said his father, 'what the magic trick was. Education, Orson! Education is your magic trick. If you don't sound impressive, you won't be impressive!'

'But Dad—'

'Just a moment, Orson,' said his dad. 'You need to understand this. Delivery, wit, presentation and showmanship. It's what makes or breaks a performer. Sets them apart from other magicians. Is your Uncle Tom funny?'

Orson didn't have to think about it. 'No.'

'Would he make a good magician?'

'No,' replied Orson, matter-of-factly.

Orson's dad nodded. 'You see what I mean, then? It takes more than technical brilliance to become a successful magician. Two magicians could perform the exact same trick. One might get a standing ovation, the other a tame round of applause. You need charisma, stage presence and showmanship to pull off illusions and tricks.'

Orson shook his head. 'I don't know what the word "charisma" even means.'

'Ah!' cried his dad, pointing his finger in the air. 'You're here now. What do you do?'

Orson took the dictionary back and leafed through it. 'Charisma is an attractiveness or charm that can inspire devotion in others,' he read after a moment.

'Now that's magic!' said Orson's father.

CHAPTER SEVEN

A Man Not Called Anthony

Ms Beresford had no charisma. Orson knew this for a fact, and he didn't need to consult his father for confirmation. He just knew it. Come to think of it, she wasn't very funny, either.

In fact, he'd never seen her smile, let alone laugh or tell a joke. Ever! Even during the weekly bingo competition on a Friday, when she was handing prizes over to the winners, he'd never seen her crack a smile.

He'd learnt a new word only yesterday: empathy. She was lacking that quality, too. The more he thought about it, the more he knew she wouldn't make a good magician.

On the other hand, Conor Murphy, the boy who sat next to him, would. He was chatty and confident and could talk his way out of a hostage situation.

Raymond Rooney, one seat further up, was a nice boy, but this admirable trait would be his downfall. Raymond always blushed when he lied, and a magician needed to be able to swindle and bluff with the best of them. A flushed face would give the game away.

Misdirection and slyness were also key components of a magician's repertoire, and Ruby Westenra, sitting by the window, was too sweet and honest. Lovely girl, mind you, and the best footballer in the class by some distance.

Returning to Ms Beresford, though! If the poor lady had the ability to teleport, vanish, hold her breath underwater for twenty minutes, turn a pig into a person, fly in the sky, read minds, control the weather, or breathe fire through her nostrils, she still wouldn't make a good magician.

Her presentation skills would be lacking. She wouldn't be able to entertain an audience. His father was right. Some people just weren't cut out to be magicians. Who else? He looked around the room, enjoying this game. How could he forget? There was also—

'Orson, put the cards away!' shrieked Ms Beresford, spotting Orson practising his card flourishes at the back of the class. 'And stop daydreaming. You'll never make anything of yourself if you keep messing about with those silly playing cards all day. Put them in your bag.'

Orson finished his card flourish.

'Put them away now, Orson!' said Ms Beresford with a sigh.

Orson did as he was asked. 'Yes, Miss.'

Ms Beresford was very clever, though, and Orson sometimes thought that there wasn't a single question in the entire world that she wouldn't know the answer to.

So, when school ended and the restless students had almost all departed for the Christmas holidays, he asked Ms Beresford what time the local library closed and was taken aback to discover that she didn't know.

Agatha Anderson, however, did know and turned to him with a smile. 'Half past six.'

Orson smiled back. What an amazing magician Agatha would make. There was just something about her. She was funny, clever, had a good personality and could lie through her teeth. Every teacher in the school liked her and she was popular among all the students, too.

She was the class representative and helped organise everything from the bingo and the parent-teacher meetings to school plays and parties. She even looked like a magician with her fashionable, red-framed glasses that suited her face and her long, flowing, jet-black hair.

As luck would have it, she was going to the library to wait for her mum, who was picking her up after work. So off they went, school bags slung over their shoulders, and began the short walk into town.

As they trudged down the red-bricked lane leading to a busy shopping district, Agatha turned to Orson. 'Why are you going to the library?' she asked him.

'To read books on magic!' replied Orson proudly.

'Really?' said Agatha. 'Like what? Give me an example.'

'Well,' replied Orson, 'I've read all the books on hypnotism, mentalism and psychology. You know, mind-reading skills and the unconscious mind.'

Agatha looked sceptical. 'I'm not sure I believe in any of that magic stuff.'

Orson groaned. 'My dad says there are two types of people in this world. Those who believe in magic and those who don't. Funnily enough, I would've had you down as a believer. Maybe you will be, one day.'

'Maybe,' said Agatha with a shy smile, pushing up her glasses.

Dressed for the cold weather, they walked on together past shops festooned with dazzling Christmas lights and garlands. When they reached the library, Orson went quietly upstairs while Agatha stayed on the ground floor in what was known as the main reading area.

Before Orson had made it to the top of the staircase, he looked down and saw that Agatha already had her nose stuck in a book. She held the book of her choosing up, but Orson couldn't make out the title. He gave a thumbs up, anyway. If Agatha was reading it, then it was definitely a good book.

Orson found himself a table in the upstairs reading area, dropped his school bag down on the floor and made his way over to a large shelf entitled 'Magic and Mystery'.

He'd already read all of the books, journals and manuscripts in the magic collection from cover to cover, so he wanted to pick a couple of books from the mystery section. Two books were quickly chosen at random and taken down from the shelf.

Another book sat slightly askew on the shelf, as if somebody had just left it there, clumsily, a few minutes ago.

Orson was about to push the book back into place, when the title caught his eye. 'Secret Societies,' he said to himself. After a moment's consideration, he reached up and took the book as well, before bringing all three books back to his table.

He sat down and studied each book. There was one on UFOs and aliens with an image of an extra-terrestrial, namely a little green man with bulbous black eyes, on the front cover.

Parked in a crop-circled field behind the alien was his favoured mode of transport around outer space – a flying saucer!

The second book was on the supposed existence of lake monsters and, on its cover, was the long neck of a prehistoric-looking dinosaur, a plesiosaur perhaps, emerging from the depths of a lake.

The book on secret societies had the symbol of a black skull on its front that, to Orson, seemed mysterious and scary.

Out of the corner of his eye, Orson spotted another like-minded individual loitering around the magic and mystery section – he was a bearded, middle-aged man, who was dressed in a black three-piece suit.

The man had curly black hair and a trim beard and, strangely, despite looking fit and healthy, he used a cane with a distinctive silver skull at its top as a crutch.

After much consideration, Orson settled on the secret societies book and, over the next half an hour, he sat and devoured the first seven chapters.

Each society covered was shrouded in mystery and legend. However, all of them shared commonalities – oaths of secrecy, a symbol unique to them, a secret handshake, hidden rituals, initiation ceremonies and covert meetings behind closed doors.

What was less clear were the motives of some of these societies. Power and money was certainly a good guess, but there were numerous conspiracy theories attached to them as well.

Some were purported to have been established in order to protect religious artefacts associated with the life of Jesus Christ. Others went on missions around the world in search of ancient artefacts in an effort to unlock their secrets and powers. Then there was a world-wide Society of Magicians.

What did they do? Flipping the page to chapter eight, Orson was just about to delve deeper into that when a loud thud broke the silence in the library.

The noise startled him. He looked across the library and observed a window wide open at the far end of the aisle, close to the magic and mystery section. What was going on? Had somebody fallen out the window?

Hurrying to the window and peering over the ledge at the drop below, Orson suddenly felt very lightheaded. This was a tall building and he was on the second floor!

With all his might, he grabbed the frame of the window and was about to close it, when a shadow materialised behind him. Turning quickly around, he saw the besuited man who had been looking for a book a little earlier, standing before him.

'Aliens?' said the man, inching closer.

Orson shook his head. 'Huh?'

The man was pointing his cane back towards the desk that Orson had been sitting at. 'Do you plan on reading the book on aliens?'

Orson had almost forgotten about the other two books on his desk. 'Not at the moment,' he replied, 'but I was thinking of bringing it home to read.'

The man's gloved hand tightened on the skull of the cane. 'You're young Whitlock, aren't you?'

Orson was stunned. 'And who are you?'

'I work here,' replied the man vaguely. 'We've had some problems recently with late book returns and the payment of overdue fines. I believe you've an outstanding fine yourself?'

Orson arched his eyebrows. 'I don't remember that. I always return my books on time.' He tried to move away from the opened window and, more importantly, the drop below. However, when he attempted to do this, the man blocked his path in a threatening manner.

The man pointed his cane out the window. 'Quite a drop.'

Orson turned. The view out the window was incredible, showcasing some of the city of London's most iconic landmarks, yet his sole focus was on the drop below. The fall to the pavement was significant. He turned back to the man and they stared at each other for a tense moment.

'I see you along this aisle quite often,' remarked the man, his eyes enlarging. 'A fellow magic enthusiast. There aren't that many of us left. As far as I'm concerned, there are two types of people in this world. Those who believe in magic and those who don't.'

'Sorry, who are you?' asked Orson again.

The man inched forward, pushing Orson perilously close to the open window.

'I'm a fellow believer, Mr Whitlock!' he proclaimed.

Orson shook his head. 'I thought you were a librarian.'

The man flashed a fake smile, the sort of smile that Orson imagined Ms Beresford might make if she ever attempted one.

'Oh, I'm a lot more than a librarian, Mr Whitlock.'

'Really?' said Orson.

'I also happen to know your father,' said the man. 'I was saddened to hear of his recent ill health. Do send my regards.'

Orson shook his head. 'My dad isn't ill.'

The man gave Orson a vacant stare. 'Is he not?'

Just then, Agatha appeared next to Orson, her arms laden with books.

'Who are you?' she said, looking up at the man. Realising she was talking too loudly, she lowered her voice to a whisper. 'You two really shouldn't be talking in the library.'

The man turned. 'I was just leaving,' he said quietly, staring at Agatha for a long moment. 'Goodbye, little miss.' Then a quick nod at Orson. 'The next time we meet, Mr Whitlock, you're going to want to speak to me.'

Agatha watched the strange man walk down the aisle and around the next corner, listening to his cane clacking on the wooden floorboards as he went.

'Gosh, I've never seen him in here before,' she said in a hushed voice. 'Who is he?'

Orson walked back to his desk. 'He works here. He wanted the book on aliens.'

'He's probably in it!' replied Agatha, walking alongside Orson.

Orson laughed. 'I'm borrowing these three,' he said, as he lifted his books from the table. He stuck a book tag on the start page of chapter eight in the book on secret societies.

Agatha cast a dismissive look at the books in Orson's hands and heaved a deep sigh when she saw the titles. 'Secret societies, aliens and lake monsters!' she said condescendingly.

Orson smiled back at her. 'What's wrong with that?'

'Interesting choices,' said Agatha sarcastically.

Orson glimpsed just one of the many books gathered in Agatha's arms and tried to stifle his laughter as he read the title. 'Marketing and Economics,' he said dismissively. 'Sounds like fun. Get the popcorn out for that one.'

Agatha rolled her eyes, but her face brightened. 'We've different tastes and interests. Let's just leave it at that. I've to go. My mum's here. I've choir practice.'

'Oh, okay,' said Orson. 'Have a lovely Christmas.'

'You too,' replied Agatha, adjusting her glasses as she waved goodbye.

Orson went to the front desk and placed his three chosen books on the counter, one on top of the other.

Ms Warren, or 'the library lady' as his mum sometimes referred to her, was finishing up a phone call, so Orson produced his dinner money change from his jacket pocket and placed it on the counter.

'Hello, Orson,' said Ms Warren as she stamped each book. 'Just to let you know that we'll be closed for the next week over Christmas.'

'Yeah, I know,' said Orson, handing over his library card.

Ms Warren smiled at him. 'So you can keep these books until the new year.' She narrowed her eyes and held up the book on secret societies. 'Is this one of ours?'

Orson nodded. 'It was in the mystery section.'

'It's not on the system,' replied Ms Warren, writing the name of the book down in a logbook. 'It's not a problem. I've it noted.'

Ms Warren switched her attention to the coins on the counter. 'What is this, Orson?'

Orson dug into his jacket pocket. 'My pocket money. I was going to pay off some of the balance on my late book. How much more do I owe?'

Ms Warren smiled, gathered the coins up on the counter and handed them back. 'You don't have any late returns, Orson.' She sought confirmation of this fact in her logbook, but her first instinct was the correct one.

'But the man who works here told me I had a fine,' said Orson, looking bewildered.

'What man?' asked Ms Warren, handing Orson back his library card.

'The man in the black suit,' said Orson. 'The new guy. He has a cane.'

Ms Warren shook her head. 'Anthony is the only man who works here. You know Anthony, don't you, Orson?'

Orson did know Anthony. It wasn't Anthony.

'Never mind,' said Ms Warren. 'You keep that money and you and your family have a lovely Christmas.'

Orson smiled and gathered up his books. 'Thank you, Ms Warren, and a Merry Christmas to you, too.'

*

After battling through the heavy city travel, Orson and his mum were home in twenty-five minutes. Rushing upstairs, he threw his school bag in the corner of his room, then went into the workshop looking for his dad, whom he discovered was away on business.

After eating his signature dish of scrambled eggs and toast, he swiped a few chocolates from the silver tray on the kitchen table, went to his room with his books under his arm and turned on his bedside light.

In no time, he was once again reading his book on secret societies, and what a chapter it was. The best of the eight by far.

Apparently, there was a world-wide secret society that had protected magicians throughout the ages. Its roots could be traced back to medieval times when witchcraft, sorcery and magic were crimes punishable by death. Later, fines or imprisonment were imposed on people who claimed to have magical powers.

To fight this, a secret society was initially set up called the Society of Magicians to protect magicians whose lives were in danger. The most powerful person in the Society of Magicians was the Grand Master, who was elected by the members.

However, over the generations, tensions soon developed and the society split into two rival groups. They had been at war ever since.

Orson read all this in amazement. He'd never known that a deck of cards or a gimmick coin could've got so many people in trouble.

If he'd been alive back in the 1500s, he too would've been in a lot of hot water for a simple card trick or a vanishing coin effect. Perhaps one of his ancestors had been in trouble back then. After all, the Whitlock name had been synonymous with magic for generations.

Popping a chocolate in his mouth, Orson observed the black skull on the front cover of the book. Was the Society of Magicians still around today to help magicians like him? His father would know more about this. He was sure of it. And he was going to ask him all about it over the Christmas holidays.

CHAPTER EIGHT

Christmas Eve, 1971

His dad was away on business for the next few days, but Orson wasn't worried. With the nature of his father's work, it was normal for him to be away for days on end, especially at this time of the year when he was always inundated with orders.

Anyway, their Christmas Eve pact was unbreakable. His dad would never miss that. Moreover, Orson knew that he would be opening his main present shortly, and thoughts of what awaited him under the Christmas tree filled him with excitement.

He lay awake, waiting for his dad to arrive. He checked his bedside clock and, when the time had just turned four o'clock and he heard footsteps pacing down the corridor, he sat up in expectation.

'Orson, are you awake?'

Orson's eyes narrowed. 'Mum?'

Grace Whitlock sat solemnly down upon her son's bed. 'Orson, I have something to tell you.' Her voice was quavering.

Orson looked curiously around. 'Where's Dad?'

'That's what I need to talk to you about, Orson,' replied his mum. 'Your father was taken ill a couple of days ago. He's in hospital. We didn't want to alarm you.'

Orson felt like he'd been punched in the gut. Words like 'sick' and 'operation' were relayed to him, along with other medical terms he didn't understand or care to. He fell into his mother's arms in tears and they held each other closely for nigh on ten minutes.

'Will you do something for me, Orson?' asked his mum.

'Anything, Mum,' replied Orson tearfully.

'Say a prayer for your dad tonight before you fall asleep,' said his mum with tears in her eyes and rosary beads in her hand.

Orson said every single prayer he knew, repeatedly, asking God to watch over and protect his father in hospital.

However, he never slept another wink until it was time to visit his father the next day in hospital. So, on Christmas Eve morning, he made sure he was up early, dressed and had his breakfast, before he and his mum left for the hospital with a Get Well Soon card and a bag of mixed grapes.

Arriving at the hospital twenty minutes later, his mum reversed the car into the nearest parking space. 'You were born in this hospital eleven years ago,' she said. 'I remember it like yesterday.'

Orson burst into tears. 'Is Daddy going to be okay?' he sobbed.

'Oh, Orson,' said his mum, leaning over and placing an arm around her son. 'He's out of surgery and the nurse I spoke to on the phone this morning said he's doing just fine.'

'Is that good?' asked Orson, wiping his eyes.

'Yes, that's good,' replied his mum with a gentle smile. 'Come on. You grab the card and I'll take the grapes.'

'I don't think Dad even likes grapes, Mum,' said Orson, lifting the card.

His mum smiled. 'Come on.'

A few minutes later they were at the main reception desk.

'This way,' said the nurse to Orson and his mum as they followed her down a corridor and into a ward.

Confronted with sickness wherever he looked, Orson kept his eyes fixed on the floor, and didn't lift them again until he heard a curtain being drawn aside and the sound of his mum's voice.

'Aren't you going to say hello to your father, Orson?' she asked.

Orson raised his eyes and saw his dad lying in bed, looking a little paler than usual. His father was dressed in a pale blue gown and had a tube in the back of his hand that ran into what appeared to be a bag of water.

'What's with the water?' asked Orson.

Martin Whitlock chuckled. 'It's not water, Orson,' he croaked.

'Does it hurt, Dad?'

'No Orson, it doesn't,' replied his dad.

'He's on a drip,' said his mum, placing the grapes on the bedside table. 'It helps replace lost fluids.'

'Never mind all that,' said Martin Whitlock. 'Come and give your father a hug. Merry Christmas, Orson.'

'Merry Christmas, Dad,' replied Orson, hugging his father.

'It's so good to see you, Orson,' said his dad.

Orson passed the card over. 'Get well soon.'

'How thoughtful,' said his dad, opening the card and reading some of the lovely messages from his family and friends.

'Will you be getting out tomorrow for Christmas Day?' asked Orson hopefully.

His dad looked back at him. 'Not just yet, Orson. It's a little too soon. But you and your mum are going to visit me tomorrow evening after dinner, and I want you to do me a favour in the meantime.'

'Anything,' replied Orson.

Martin Whitlock turned to his wife with a smile. 'Sweetheart, any chance you could pop downstairs to the shop and get me a newspaper?'

Grace Whitlock laughed heartily. 'I'll give you boys some time to yourselves.' She slid the curtain across the railing and left.

Martin Whitlock sat up. 'When you go home this evening,' he said excitedly, 'I want you to open your present under the tree. It can't wait until morning. I think you're ready. No, I *know* you're ready!'

Orson was hanging on his father's every word. 'Ready for what?' he asked rapidly.

Orson's father lowered his voice to a whisper as they could hear the footsteps of a nurse approaching. 'You'll see tonight.'

Orson glanced over his shoulder and saw the nurse's silhouette standing outside the curtain. 'Quickly, Dad. Tell me!'

His dad shook his head. 'As soon as you return home! All will be revealed!'

The curtain was drawn aside and a small nurse with a kind face and a pleasant smile entered. 'Oh, I'm sorry young man. I didn't know you were in here. I just need to check your father's blood pressure.'

'That's okay,' replied Orson.

The affable nurse wrapped a cuff around Martin Whitlock's upper arm and inflated it using a small hand pump.

Orson watched all this with interest. 'What's that?'

'A sphygmomanometer,' replied the nurse.

'A spy-a-meter?' said Orson.

The nurse laughed. 'Let's just call it a blood pressure cuff.' After declaring that Mr Whitlock's blood pressure was perfectly fine, the nurse went to leave.

'How's he doing?' asked Orson, stopping the nurse in her tracks.

'He's doing very well,' the nurse replied, turning back. 'Your dad just needs plenty of rest now.'

Grace Whitlock returned with the newspaper. 'Okay, we'll only stay ten more minutes.'

Ten more minutes, however, turned into three glorious hours as Orson and his mum sat around the hospital bed and recollected stories with his dad on cherished memories of old.

As it was Christmas Eve, the medical staff seemed to accept a certain relaxation of protocols and rules. However, when the lights were turned down and it began to snow heavily outside, the family reunions in the ward broke up and loved ones said their goodbyes.

Orson and his mum, the last to leave, promised to return on Christmas Day and to replace the card and grapes with pudding and some chocolates.

'Some chocolates!' his dad exclaimed. 'What do you mean "some chocolates"? Bring the box!'

'There mightn't be many chocolates left in the box by this time tomorrow, Dad,' predicted Orson.

Orson's mum laughed. 'Come down in a minute, Orson. Your dad needs his rest now.' She turned and left.

Orson's dad grabbed him by the hand. 'Say it, Orson. Say it and mean it.'

'I believe in magic,' said Orson staunchly.

His dad was sleepy looking now. 'You're ready. As soon as you get home. Open your present!'

Orson waited for his dad to drift off to sleep before he left.

For the last few hours, he'd been wondering what exactly was waiting for him under the Christmas tree. It was obviously a secret that his dad had held close to his chest all these years, but why? What was it?

These thoughts and many more troubled him greatly as he joined his mum in the car to begin the journey home. The snow lingered in the air as his mum drove to a busy Christmas market to pick up some last-minute gifts for the neighbours and, thereafter, to their parish church to say a prayer before the crib of Bethlehem.

As he knelt in the pew, Orson could hear the choir high above him rehearsing for midnight mass. As he offered up a prayer for his dad and all the sick people in hospital on this Christmas Eve night, he listened to classic hymns like 'O Little Town of Bethlehem', 'Away in a Manger', 'The First Noel' and 'Silent Night' reverberating around the great walls of the church.

Just as Orson and his mum were contemplating leaving, Agatha walked past them and ascended the steps onto the altar to rehearse 'O Holy Night'.

They sat back down and Agatha sang the famous hymn with such glorious aplomb and accomplishment that Grace Whitlock had tears rolling down her cheeks by the end.

When Agatha had finished, a round of applause went up and, although only half a dozen people were present in the church, the noise they made mirrored a hundred.

Orson led the applause and he watched Agatha closely as she made her way down from the altar and along the aisle. He caught her eye as she went past and they smiled at each other.

'Do you know that girl?' asked his mum curiously.

Orson was still clapping. 'She's in my class.'

'A girlfriend of yours?' asked his mum with a faint smile.

Orson rolled his eyes, stopped clapping and peered up at his mum. 'What do you reckon, Mum?'

To see his mum smiling again, even at his own expense, thrilled Orson no end.

'Let's go,' said his mum. 'Before we're snowed in the church for the night!'

They walked past the crib of Bethlehem and Orson saw his mum take a piece of straw from beside the baby Jesus on their way out.

By the time they arrived back home, Orson could think of nothing other than his present under the Christmas tree, but the opportunity to open it was proving rather tricky.

After helping to bring the shopping bags in and place all the contents in the fridge and cupboards, he was assigned to hoover the floor and wash the dishes.

When he tried to excuse himself, his mum would allocate something else to be hoovered up, while she made final adjustments to a few golden angels that hung lopsidedly on the Christmas tree.

Unplugging the hoover, Orson followed his mum into the living room. At least he was edging closer to the tree and to the great secret that lay underneath it.

'What time are we visiting Dad tomorrow?' asked Orson, his eyes on the presents.

'Any time after three,' replied his mum, picking up her car keys from the coffee table.

Orson's mum turned fully around to look at him. 'Orson, you do know that your grandad and grandma are still coming for dinner tomorrow?'

Orson nodded.

'After dinner, we'll all head to the hospital to visit your dad,' said his mum. 'One of my brothers might be calling around for dinner, too.'

Orson smiled. 'Oh, really? Uncle Brian might be coming?'

Orson's mum shook her head. 'Your Uncle Tom, actually.'

'Oh, right,' replied Orson. His eager eyes were back on the presents under the tree. 'Anything else I can help with?'

'Mmm, good question,' said his mum, looking around the living room. 'Well, I suppose the carpet could do with a hoovering. You didn't unplug the hoover, I hope?'

'More hoovering?' said Orson, raising his eyebrows. 'Gosh, Mum, there's only so much excitement a kid can take on Christmas Eve.'

Grace Whitlock laughed. 'I'm heading out. I've an appointment with my hairdresser, and then I've to call to the butchers in town to collect the ham for tomorrow. Would you like to come for the drive?'

Orson shook his head and drew his breath, trying to hide his excitement at the prospect of his mum's imminent departure. 'I'll be okay here, Mum.'

'You're sure?' asked his mum.

Orson nodded. 'Of course.'

His mum switched on the television and handed the newspaper, open on the Christmas Eve channel listings, to Orson. 'TV should be good, Orson. Lots of movies on. I'll be home in an hour. Don't be bored.'

'I won't be,' said Orson, scanning the channel listings. It wasn't until his mum's car had pulled out of the avenue and the headlights had diminished that Orson knew that he'd the house to himself.

Barely able to contain his excitement, he threw the newspaper down on the couch and hurried out to the conservatory, where the tree stood in all its wondrous glory.

Outside, it was dark and cold. The snowflakes were continuing to fall and, while this would've filled him with joy at any other time, he simply noted the fact to himself and got down on his knees.

Given that it was almost five o'clock on Christmas Eve, the presents had mounted up, even since yesterday when he had come down to have a quick peek at them.

He checked the large presents first, his eyes desperately searching for a tag that read *To Orson, From Dad*. The larger presents were ruled out quickly and, as for the smaller ones, they were all to his mum from her three sisters and two brothers.

Out of respect, he checked the gift tags carefully before returning each present to the foot of the tree, in the exact same position that he had found them.

When he eventually found his own present, hiding between two larger parcels, he raised it into the air as if he'd unearthed a hidden jewel.

The present was shaped like a shoe box and up he held it, the lights of the tree illuminating the blue and white wrapping paper.

Even with trembling hands, he managed to untie the golden ribbons holding it all together.

The lid was quickly raised and he peered in.

CHAPTER NINE

The Centre of Excellence

The first item Orson removed from the box was a white envelope with his name scribbled on the front of it. Underneath his name, written with a lot more care, were the words *For your urgent attention.*

Next, he took from the box four more white envelopes, each one embossed with a different-coloured skull. He ran back into the living room and laid all the envelopes out on the carpet. He had to figure this out.

Opening the envelope that was addressed to him, he removed a slip of paper, unfolded it, and began to read. 'Merry Christmas, Orson. Congratulations on making it this far. I never made it to this stage at your age. So good luck, I hope you can do it! You must choose one envelope. Just one, and follow the instructions on it. May all your dreams come true. Love, Dad.'

Orson put the card down and spread all four envelopes out, side by side, on the carpet before him, as if he were about to perform a magic trick. He studied each one and his eyes went back and forth along the line many times over.

The skulls on the front of each envelope were blue, black, green and red and showed up very clearly against the white backdrop. He wiggled his fingers over each envelope, trying to decipher any subtle difference in them, but they were all the same proportions.

And yet, his first instinct was the envelope with the black skull. If he hadn't read the book on secret societies, he might've regarded all four envelopes the same; but the colour black symbolised secrets and mysteries and that was a strong enough hunch for him to work on.

Lifting the envelope that was embossed with the black skull, he turned it over and unsealed it. He took a moment to compose himself.

He would be inconsolable if he was wrong, but he'd obey his father's wishes regardless. No matter how much willpower he would have to call upon, he would open this *one* envelope and no other.

He peeled it open. Inside, there was a note and he read it aloud. 'Congratulations Orson, you've chosen wisely. I want you to go to my workshop and bring last year's Christmas present with you.'

Orson was gobsmacked. The English dictionary? He ran out the door of the living room, along the corridor and upstairs into his bedroom.

On the last day of school, he'd flung his school bag into the corner of his room, fully expecting it to stay there, without disturbance, until the new year.

Rummaging around, he saw all fifty-two cards of his spare deck scattered around the bottom of his school bag. It didn't take him long to discover the dictionary lodged between his maths and geography textbooks.

Holding the dictionary, he bounded down the stairs, sprinted along the corridor and hurried into his father's workshop, opening and closing the door as quickly as he could.

The lights were off, so he heard the ticking of the clocks before he saw them. Flicking on the lights, he saw old, new and recently restored clocks hanging everywhere he looked.

There were blueprints and instructions for numerous clocks, not yet made, stacked on shelves. In the corner of the room stood a lathe, a machine Orson knew his father used for furbishing parts.

He walked past a cabinet equipped with hammers and many different types of saws, all the time wondering how an English dictionary could possibly be needed in a workshop like this. Then he spotted a bookshelf in the room. This was promising.

There were books on a whole range of topics from geography and travel to woodwork and clockmaking. However, what really caught his eye were books on hypnotism, trance states and secret societies.

And what was this?! Orson's eyes shot open. An entire area of the shelf was devoted to dictionaries. He ran his finger along the line.

'French, Spanish, Italian,' he said with narrowed eyes. There was a gap, then a German dictionary. *No* English one. He smiled and placed the English dictionary into the gap, hearing the bookshelf click open a moment later.

A blast of freezing cold air blew through the gap as Orson pulled the frame of the shelf back to reveal a hidden passageway. In he walked, poised for anything.

The passageway was so dark and dismal that he left the bookshelf ajar so that he could see where he was walking. Even then, visibility was difficult.

Nevertheless, the sliver of light did reveal a spiral staircase up ahead. He advanced towards it and groped his way up, listening to each footstep echoing.

There was a speck of light, like a twinkling star, above his head and he kept his eye upon this as he scaled the steps.

Reaching the top, his legs hit a trip wire, the kind he often saw in films, which usually triggered a bomb or a flurry of poisoned darts.

In this case, it caused instantaneous change as gold confetti began to fall from the ceiling like snowflakes. Slow and sporadic at first, then faster and more plentiful, until Orson couldn't see anything but gold flakes before his eyes.

There was nothing else for it; he had to stand still, as the sheer volume of the confetti was too great. Raising his arms, he shut his eyes and peered upwards, enjoying the softness of the confetti on his face. He couldn't help but laugh.

When the deluge finally neared the end and the ribbons began to descend more intermittently, Orson began to walk forward again.

He was standing on a lofty balcony and went quickly towards the balustrade. Stretching his neck out, he peered down.

It was a feast for the eyes with wonders everywhere he looked. He found himself overlooking another workshop, but instead of containing clocks it had been converted into a museum of magical excellence. There was an assortment of all the greatest gadgets and gismos ever invented by some of the best minds in magic.

Everywhere he turned, he saw state-of-the-art props, effects and magic inventory that any performer in the world would love to get their hands on.

Even from a fair height up, Orson recognised some of the inventory from magic shows that he'd seen on the television. He needed to get down there to inspect them further.

One step at a time, he began to climb down the ladder linking the balcony to the workshop and, when he got near the bottom, he slid down the rest of the way.

Just by scanning the workshop, Orson could tell that it was meticulously planned into different categories. As he walked further inside, he saw a long and narrow book-lined aisle with shelves stacked from A to Z with handsome books on all things magic, mentalism and mystery.

Some of the books in the library were antique editions read by only a select few magicians throughout history. The secrets contained within these rare editions were never disclosed, and Orson realised that some of the most important books ever written on magic were to be found on these shelves.

There were long aisles that rounded corners, stretching further than his eye could see. There was a clothes department with rails hung with beautifully tailored three-piece suits, pristine black capes, cutaway coats, bow ties of varying colours, white gloves and top hats. Mesmerised, he continued with his tour of the workshop.

There were two large, dimly lit glass cabinets full of wands, perhaps twenty in each display, and every single one of them was unique in their craftmanship.

To his left, he saw straightjackets, keys, locks, empty water tanks, fishbowls, swords, fake saws, real saws, magnets, lockets, crystal balls, secret cabinets, magic pens, metal-plated watches, invisible ink cartridges and transporting coins.

To his right, he saw bottles of fake blood, balloons, double-sided adhesive tape, trapdoors, reels of invisible thread, innumerable packets of flash paper, sledgehammers, watches, magnetic gold rings, and countless decks of magnificently crafted playing cards that were displayed like jewellery inside a glass cabinet.

Then there was an area allocated to equipment that looked better suited to some terrible torture chamber than a magical workshop. Orson fixed his eyes on a wooden table with ominous-looking metal spikes protruding from it, and quite nearby was a platform with razor-sharp nails.

And, if all these horrors weren't enough, over by the corner, half-hidden by a red cloth, was a fearsome-looking guillotine. Whether this instrument of death was real or not, Orson could not say. Nor did he wish to know!

On he went. A few steps in any direction brought new sights.

There were wooden boxes of every shape and size that surely doubled as some sort of deviously deceptive prop, all of them ingeniously engineered by his father.

The scope of his dad's vision was breathtaking. What an extraordinary place his father had assembled! It was a shrine to all things magic.

Given all the extensive resources, materials and intricately designed equipment gathered, this workshop had obviously been years, if not decades, in the making. Orson knew one thing for certain – it would help to elevate his magic to the next level.

Up next was a display of the most realistic-looking collection of rubber masks he'd ever seen. If he ever took the notion to disguise himself as a bearded man of sixty years of age, he now had the means to do so.

There were fake moustaches, ears, noses, wigs, and an array of body suits that could alter his appearance to such a degree that his own mum wouldn't recognise him.

Walking down a different aisle, Orson discovered another display cabinet with black canes hanging up. He'd seen one of these canes before. The man whom he'd met in the library had one. With narrowed eyes, he went closer and observed the distinctive silver skull at the top of each cane.

Next to this cabinet was a gallery of framed posters and photographs. Above them, upon the wall, a motto was written. Casting his eyes upwards, Orson read the words aloud. 'There are two types of people in this world. Those who believe in magic and those who don't.'

Orson walked along, looking at the posters, predominately from a bygone era, that had been enlarged and restored to their former glories.

One such poster depicted an illustration of an escape artist, upside down inside a water tank, while another showed a magician holding a crystal ball, as if she were about to reveal the secrets of the universe to the assembled crowd.

Then there was the collection of photographs of varying sizes hung on the walls.

Of particular interest to Orson was a photograph of his father and grandfather and one other man. His jaw dropped.

All three men were well-dressed in navy suits and red bow ties and, in their hands, they clasped black canes with skulls at their tops.

It was very strange for Orson to see both his father and grandfather looking so well groomed. They both had more hair on their heads and fewer wrinkles on their faces, and he guessed this picture was taken maybe thirty years ago.

The other man was younger, but even he looked vaguely familiar somehow. Orson fixed his eyes upon him. It was the man from the library.

The man was merely a teenager when this photo was taken, but it was him. Orson was sure of it. So his father and grandfather knew this man! Who was he? How did his father and grandfather know him? What was the connection?

His father was obviously a member of the Society of Magicians. No further proof was needed. What's more, if the book he read in the library was correct, then the society was originally set up to protect magicians whose lives were in danger. Was this still the case? Orson had so many questions.

When he visited his dad tomorrow in hospital, he would try his best to start finding out some answers.

CHAPTER TEN

Christmas Day, 1971

When Christmas dinner was over the next day, Orson assisted with the washing-up before dessert was served. There were choices. Orson picked the sherry trifle that his mum had spent the last day or so making. His decision was based solely on the fact that it was always simply delicious.

The apple pie was warmed in the oven and Orson carried over a healthy slice each for his grandad and grandma. Uncle Tom, after some consideration, had the strawberry cheesecake. Grace Whitlock brought over the jug of hot custard from the kitchen counter, together with a bowl of her own sherry trifle, and took her place at the table.

The whipped cream was passed around, and everyone added a couple of spoonfuls to their chosen dessert. After the coffee was served and the chocolates were brought out, everyone sat around talking.

'What a delicious Christmas dinner, Grace,' said Tom. 'Thank you.'

Orson's grandfather and grandmother both agreed, saying it was even better than last year, which they didn't think possible beforehand. What wasn't better, however, was the vacant chair at the dinner table.

'How's the patient doing?' asked Francis L. Whitlock.

Grace Whitlock couldn't hide her relief. 'Much better, I'm happy to say!' She topped up everyone's drinks – a double brandy for grandad, a sherry for grandma, a lemonade for Uncle Tom and a glass of chocolate milk for Orson.

'And a bottle of beer for the patient,' said Orson's grandfather, taking a bottle from the fridge. 'I can't forget my son on Christmas Day.'

Orson's mum tutted. 'Frank, he's on medication. Besides, you can't bring a bottle of beer into a hospital! You'll get us thrown out! Would you like that to happen?'

'Nobody will see it!' said Orson's grandfather, winking at Orson. He pulled a silk cloth from his pocket, wrapped it around the bottle and said, 'Alakazam!'

Orson laughed when the bottle vanished.

Usually, they'd all retire to the living room after dinner and watch a film on television, but this was no ordinary Christmas Day and, instead, conversations were cut short as they found their coats and scarfs in the hot press. Everyone was ready within five minutes.

Braving the hard frost, Orson led everyone outside. He walked alongside his grandma to the car and kept a firm hand on her elbow, just to make sure she didn't slip on the frosty ground.

Then he found the sweeping brush by the side of the house and cleared snow off the front and back car screens. His mum was the last of all to leave and, when she had closed all the windows, turned off the Christmas tree lights and locked the front door, they were on their way.

Ever since his discovery of the magic workshop, Orson had been wondering when he would get the chance to speak to his father again. He still pondered this question as they journeyed to the hospital.

It would be next to impossible to ask his dad a single question with everyone else present. He had so many questions. Who was the man in the photograph? Did the Society of Magicians exist? And, if so, was his father a member?

Given it was the early evening of Christmas Day, the roads were quiet. However, it wasn't long into the journey when Orson suddenly noticed that his grandfather was acting very strangely.

For whatever reason, Grandad Frank couldn't sit still. It was a seldom sight indeed to see a car appear behind them, but when one did, Orson's grandad would turn around and peer out the back window suspiciously.

Orson obviously wasn't the only person to notice this, as his mum, who was sitting in the passenger seat, turned around. 'Everything all right back there, Frank?' she asked.

Francis L. Whitlock moved to the edge of his seat, restless. 'I think someone is tailing us.'

Uncle Tom clasped the steering wheel. 'What? The police? I wasn't speeding!'

Grandad Frank erupted into a fit of laughter. 'We know that, Tom!'

Grace Whitlock turned right around and looked sceptically at her father-in-law. 'Nobody is following us, Frank. What would make you think that?'

'Many things, Grace,' replied her father-in-law. 'I've many reasons to believe that someone might be following us. I'll be more specific. A black Rolls-Royce has been behind us since the last set of lights. I'm sure of it.'

Orson's grandma looked incredulous, too. 'Francis, you're imagining things!' She rummaged in her handbag. 'And you forgot to take your tablets before you left.'

'Just a moment, Alice,' interjected Orson's mum. 'Frank has had a few drinks. Maybe he shouldn't be taking his medication.'

Frank smiled. 'Grace is right, honey. I'd be asleep in two minutes.' He leant forward. 'C'mon, Tom, it's not a tractor you're driving!'

'Huh?' said Tom.

'Give it some welly, man!' cried Frank. 'The roads are quiet. The poor old boy in hospital will think we're not coming at this rate. I'm in a bad way for the toilet, too! Step on it!'

'Nice and steady does it,' replied Tom indignantly. 'I'm going at the speed limit, Francis.'

'So you are,' said Orson's grandfather with a sigh. 'So you are.'

Orson sat quietly in the back, practising his double lifts with his deck of cards.

'How's the magic coming along, Orson?' asked Tom, spotting him.

Orson's face broke into a smile. 'I just love it! I practise every day for hours and read loads of magic books. I honestly can't stop thinking about it, Tom!'

Tom smiled as he stopped at a set of lights. 'I'm delighted for you. If you're half as good a magician as your dad and…cover your husband's ears please, Alice.'

Alice complied, placing her hands over her husband's ears.

'…or, indeed, your grandfather,' Tom went on, 'then you might be able to earn a pretty good living out of it.'

'Did I miss something?' asked Orson's grandfather, grinning from ear to ear when his dear wife of forty-nine years had removed her hands from over his ears.

A car horn honked.

'Green light, Tom,' said Grace.

'Oh, right,' said Tom, moving off.

'Did you ever think of going into magic, Tom?' asked Orson, which made his grandfather smother a laugh.

Tom sighed. 'No, Orson. I did get hypnotised once, though, and by all accounts I was made to look a little foolish. Jumping around like a chicken or something.'

Orson laughed.

Tom looked at his nephew through the rear-view mirror. 'I was always more interested in numbers and accounts,' he told him. 'Tax returns and that sort of thing. Balance sheets, budget forecasts and preparing financial statements. Can I tell you an accounting story from work, Orson? Quite exciting.'

'Sure,' said Orson sincerely.

'Goodness me!' cried Frank, guffawing. 'Pass me those tablets after all, Alice, my dear!'

Alice jabbed her husband in the ribs. 'Stop it, Francis!'

Grace Whitlock turned around. 'You've had far too much to drink, Francis,' she admonished. 'You really have. At this rate, you'll embarrass us all in the hospital.'

Francis L. Whitlock held his hands up defensively. 'I'll behave. I promise.'

Orson's mum wasn't so sure. 'I'm beginning to think we should've left you in the armchair at home to sleep it off. Tom was kind enough to drive us to the hospital.'

'You're right, Grace,' said Orson's grandfather with a grin. 'My apologies, Tom. I'm just teasing. What can I say? It's Christmas Day! I'm in a jovial mood. You're very kind to drive us and you're an excellent accountant. You kept my tax in order for many years, and for that I'm very grateful!'

'Thanks, Francis,' said Tom.

Frank nodded. 'What's more, I can scarcely wait to hear your accounting story. Carry on please, sir. Regale us all with your joyous tale.'

Alas, the joyous tale would have to wait, as Orson saw the gates of the hospital up ahead. When Uncle Tom had driven up the driveway and parked his car, everyone jumped out.

Slipping his deck of cards into his jacket pocket, Orson walked alongside his grandfather, who was still smiling like a clown about to enter the circus tent.

'Orson,' said his grandfather quietly, turning to him, 'when we're in your dad's ward, try and get the ladies to leave. Your dad and I need to speak to you alone. It's important.'

This was music to Orson's ears. He wanted to hear the truth, whatever that was. 'Okay, it's about magic, isn't it?'

The entrance doors slid open and his grandfather smiled down at him. 'Of course it's about magic!'

'What about Tom?' asked Orson. 'Can he stay, too?'

'Let me worry about your uncle!' replied Grandad Frank, heading off in the direction of the toilets.

Knowing the way to his father's ward from his previous visit, Orson led everyone up the stairs with the promised pudding in one hand and the box of chocolates in the other.

After signing in at reception, Orson was informed that his dad had been transferred to another ward.

As they made their way along a different corridor, Orson learnt from his uncle that the ward that they were walking towards was a step-down facility within the hospital.

In other words, it was a place where people who were recovering from an operation would go when they had improved. In short, it was good news!

They walked through two sets of double doors that led into a dimly lit ward and Orson couldn't help noticing the difference.

For a start, the current ward had a Christmas tree and there were families and friends mingling around the beds of their loved ones. It was clearly more relaxed and there was even a radio playing some festive music in the corner, too.

Encouraged, Orson walked on and, when the curtains were drawn aside by the nurse and he saw his father sitting up in bed looking hale and hearty, he felt a great sense of relief.

'I thought you'd never come,' said his dad, eyes on Orson and then on the box of chocolates in his son's hand.

Orson rolled his eyes. 'Who? Me or the chocolates, Dad?'

'Well, both!' replied his dad, laughing.

'Detained by the dish washing!' said Orson's grandad, rather unconvincingly.

Martin Whitlock grinned. 'You, washing dishes, Dad! I believe in miracles at Christmas, but that's stretching it a bit.'

Grace Whitlock laughed and kissed her husband. 'Merry Christmas. Glad you're feeling better, darling.'

'Merry Christmas, Grace!' replied Martin Whitlock. 'You got your hair done, honey. I like it.'

Orson observed a tray sitting upon his dad's lap with the remnants of a turkey and ham dinner.

'Merry Christmas, Martin,' said Grandma Alice, planting a kiss on her son's cheek.

'Merry Christmas, Mum. You're looking great.'

Alice patted her son twice on the arm, then lifted the tray away and left it on a side table. 'Good to see your appetite is back.'

Orson's dad gazed up from his bed. 'So good to see you all. Thanks, Tom, for driving.'

Tom was pulling up chairs by the bed. 'Not a problem, Martin.' He hung his overcoat up. 'I'm just glad to see you looking so healthy and well.'

'How are you feeling, son?' asked Frank.

Orson's dad flashed a smile. 'Yeah, quite good, Dad. I'm getting there. I'll be up and about again in no time, my doctor has assured me.'

Orson smiled when he saw what looked like a secret handshake between his dad and grandad, all but confirming his suspicions.

Francis L. Whitlock whisked a bottle of beer from behind his back and offered it to his son. 'For you!'

Martin Whitlock nearly fell out of his bed. 'Dad, you can't bring alcohol into a hospital. I can't drink that! I'm on medication.'

Grandad Frank grinned, his pearly whites gleaming. 'I was hoping you'd say that!' He opened the bottle and took a squig. 'Your health, son! Cheers!'

They all sat around and traded stories on past family Christmases, while making their way through the second layer of the chocolate box.

It was almost seven o'clock when the gathering was interrupted by a nurse, who strongly hinted that the patient should be allowed to get some rest.

Orson's mum went to the bathroom, while his grandmother made her way across the ward to visit another lady, whom she knew from her days working as a nurse in a London hospital.

Frank rubbed his hands together. 'At last. Magic, my good men. Magic! We don't have much time!'

'What's all this about then?' asked Tom, looking confused.

Orson's grandfather jumped. 'Tom, I think it would be a good idea for you to start the car before we were off, don't you? It's freezing out there, and the very thought of Alice sitting in that cold car of yours makes me shudder.'

Tom took the hint and pointed his finger in the air. 'Good idea, Francis,' he said, leaving the three generations of Whitlocks to talk amongst themselves.

Martin Whitlock sat up with a groan. Orson lifted his chair closer to the bed and his grandfather pulled the curtain.

'We don't have much time,' said Francis L. Whitlock in a low voice, laying a hand on Orson's shoulder. 'Young man, I believe you were let in on a family secret yesterday. What did you think of the Centre of Excellence?'

Orson narrowed his eyes.

'The magic workshop,' said Orson's father, seeing his son's confusion.

Orson's eyes lit up. 'It's incredible!' he replied. 'I can't wait to get back down there.'

'Well, it's all yours,' said his grandad. 'Your dad and I wanted to wait until your eighteenth birthday, but recent events have forced our hands. We've had to bring our plans forward.'

Orson nodded and told his father and grandfather that he knew about the Society of Magicians and that they were members.

His dad smiled. 'We're not just members, Orson.'

Orson rose to his feet with a smile and pointed at his dad. 'I knew it!' he cried. 'I just knew it. You're the Grand Master.'

Orson's dad refuted the suggestion immediately. 'I'm not the Grand Master, Orson,' he said with a shake of his head.

Orson turned his gaze to his grandfather.

'Don't look at me, Orson,' said his grandfather with a shrug. 'I'm retired.'

Orson shook his head. 'Then who *is* the Grand Master?'

'You, Orson!' said his father, raising a finger and pointing at his only child. 'You are!'

CHAPTER ELEVEN

An Incident at Work

Orson turned white. 'I am! What? How could I be?'

Just then, rapid footsteps could be heard on the tiled floor.

'There's something else,' said Orson's dad. 'Even more important!'

Orson frowned. He'd just discovered that he was the Grand Master of the Society of Magicians, and yet there was something even more pressing to be relayed to him. His mind boggled.

'What else?' he asked.

The footsteps drew nearer.

'Did you see a photograph in the workshop?' asked his grandfather quickly.

Orson knew exactly where this was headed. 'Yes. That was my next question. Who is the man in the photograph with both of you?'

'Grandad will tell you later,' said his dad. 'It's important.'

'Later?' cried Orson. 'Tell me now, Grandad!'

The curtain drew back and in walked Uncle Tom, rubbing his hands together to warm them.

'You were spot on, Francis. Cold out there.'

Grandad Frank threw his hands in the air. 'That was quick, wasn't it, Tom?'

'Forgot my keys!' replied Tom, finding them in the pocket of his coat.

'What's wrong, Grandma?' asked Orson, when his grandmother appeared from behind the curtains with tears in her eyes.

'It's Fionnuala,' she said solemnly.

'Who's Fionnuala?' cried Orson's grandad.

'My friend that I used to work with,' replied Alice, dabbing her eyes with her handkerchief. 'She fell off a ladder putting up decorations last week and broke her ankle! She had an operation a few days ago. Isn't that just terrible, Orson?'

'It is, Grandma,' said Orson sympathetically.

A nurse walked in carrying a clipboard under her arm. 'Sorry to interrupt, Martin,' she said, 'but it's time to take your tablets.' She checked her watch, noted the time and scribbled it down on the board. Then she handed him a plastic tub with two tablets inside.

The nurse left with a kind smile, but the ward had become quiet and everyone knew that they had overstayed their welcome.

Orson's mum came in, rounded everyone up and said it was time to go. As Orson's dad swallowed his tablets with a glass of water, everyone put on their coats and scarfs.

'Go mbeirimíd beo ar an am seo arís,' said Grace Whitlock.

Orson smiled. 'What does that mean, Mum?' he asked.

'May we all be alive at this time next year,' replied his mum.

'And not in a hospital,' said Orson's dad from his sick bed, and everyone laughed.

'Well said, Grace,' cried Francis L. Whitlock. 'Very well said indeed.'

'Irish is such a beautiful language,' said Orson. 'Why did you leave Ireland, Mum?'

'I got a job opportunity in England.'

Orson's dad chuckled. 'I thought it was because you met me?'

Orson's mum burst out laughing. 'That's the version you like to tell yourself.'

Martin Whitlock continued. 'I met your mother, Orson, when I was on summer holidays in County Donegal. She was from a parish called Tydavnet in County Monaghan.'

'My maiden name is McCormack,' said Grace Whitlock.

'I know that, Mum,' said Orson. 'Grandad and Grandma McCormack are always very kind to me whenever we visit.'

'Anyway,' said Orson's dad, 'we stayed in contact. I'd visit your mother in Ireland from time to time and she'd come over on the boat to see me. Finally, your mum made her move to England permanent in 1956. We were married just over a year later.'

Alice had tears in her eyes again. Happy ones, this time. 'How lovely.'

'We better go,' said Orson's mum, 'before they throw us out.'

There were warm goodbyes exchanged and a few hugs and kisses. Soon, however, Orson was once again helping his grandmother along the frosted footpath outside and into the back seat of the car.

Such was the cold, they all kept their coats on as the car started up.

Grace Whitlock, sitting once again in the passenger seat, turned on the heater, seatbelts were quickly fastened, and they were headed home in no time.

She put on a cassette tape and everyone sat quietly, listening to a collection of Christmas hits that Tom had recorded off the radio over the years.

As 'The Christmas Song' by Nat King Cole began to play, Orson rested his head back on the car seat and thought about what he should do next.

His grandparents would be dropped off at their house soon, so he didn't have much time to ask any further questions about the mystery man in the photograph.

He was just about to turn to his grandfather and ask him about the man in question, when Uncle Tom turned the volume down on the radio and smiled back at Orson through the rear-view mirror.

'I didn't quite get the chance to share my story earlier,' he said happily.

Grandad Frank held out his hand and Grandma Alice promptly placed two tablets in it.

Orson forced a smile. 'No time like the present, Tom.'

Uncle Tom nodded. 'I was undertaking the end of year profit and loss accounts for the company,' he said drearily, 'but the fax machine wasn't working properly. Important point to remember – it was around half past five and I had to send the accounts over to my manager before six o'clock.'

Orson looked over at his grandfather, who was rolling his eyes and shaking his head in frustration, as though he'd foreseen this situation unfolding. The septuagenarian put the two tablets, supplied by his good wife, into his mouth.

Tom continued, 'So Brendan told me—'

'Who's Brendan?' asked Orson, feigning interest.

Tom nodded. 'Brendan is a good friend of mine. He works in accounts as well. Team leader, actually. Nice guy. You'd like him. Anyway, Brendan told me that there was a fax machine in the human resource department and that, critically, it worked perfectly. You've heard of a fax machine, haven't you, Orson?'

'Oh, yes,' said Orson.

Tom smiled. 'They're incredible inventions, really. The future of modern technology. I can send a letter or document to another fax machine anywhere in the world in about six minutes. They're very popular in offices now.'

Orson nodded. 'So, did you get the accounts over in time?'

His uncle grimaced. 'Well, that's the thing. The stakes were quite high at this point, so I printed out the accounts and ran down as fast as I could to…'

As Uncle Tom continued with the story, Orson looked at his grandfather, who was sound asleep. He looked past the snoring Francis L. Whitlock and out the window. The stars were sparkling in the sky and it was a beautiful Christmas night. Snow was upon the ground and it was freezing hard.

'Had you a good Christmas Day, Orson?' his mum asked him, after turning fully around and smiling at him.

'Brilliant,' Orson muttered back, his uncle's story continuing in the background. 'Did you, Mum?'

His mum nodded and her smile grew wider. 'Not over yet, of course! You seemed to be having a great chat with your dad and grandad in the hospital. What were you all talking about?'

Orson sighed. 'Oh, nothing much.' *Nothing much!* he thought. He was the Grand Master of the Society of Magicians! Surely, it was a mistake? He still had so many questions, and every single one of them would have to wait until his dad had returned home from hospital.

Before Orson arrived home, however, one question was finally answered. His uncle *did* get the urgent fax sent over in the nick of time and disaster was averted, thanks to the human resource department and, of course, Brendan, whom Tom modestly considered the hero of the tale.

Orson, however, said he believed his uncle was the real hero of the story!

Unaccustomed to compliments, Tom reddened. 'Well, I don't know about that,' he replied humbly.

Orson found himself smiling.

A few minutes later, Orson watched his grandparents enter their house, safe in the knowledge that he would see them again on New Year's Eve.

'Thanks for sharing your fax machine story,' said Orson to his uncle, when the sight of their own house came into view five miles further on. 'And thanks also for driving us to the hospital.'

Tom parked outside the house. 'Don't mention it, Orson. Have a lovely night, and good luck with the magic.'

Orson was under no illusions. He knew he needed all the luck in the world with the magic. He waited for his mum by the threshold of the house. It was very dark.

The lights of the Christmas tree were off, which seemed an awful shame on Christmas Day, but he'd switch them on again when his mum opened the door.

The Morgans next door had their lights on and he found himself looking through their window, admiring their glittering Christmas tree for a moment. But it was no night for standing still.

Pacing up and down to keep warm, he blew out his cheeks, watching as the cold air flew like smoke from his lips. He kicked the snow, thinking.

If he was indeed the Grand Master, then in essence he was the leader of the entire magic community in England. Was he *really* the boss of thousands of magicians? It seemed absurd.

He scratched his head. At the age of eleven, he couldn't possibly be the Grand Master of the Society of Magicians. Could he?

CHAPTER TWELVE

The Grand Master's Pin

'Yes, you could!' answered Orson's father bluntly, two days later in the Centre of Excellence when that very same question was posed to him. He pushed his wheelchair forward. 'Here, let me show you.'

Orson followed his dad over to a rug embossed with a magic wand. His dad rolled it back to reveal a trapdoor. He looked across at Orson. 'You'll have to do the rest.'

Getting down on his knees, Orson pulled open the trapdoor and discovered a black box lying inside. 'What's this?'

'It's a mystery box,' replied his father.

Orson studied the box and smiled. 'It's beautiful. What's in it?'

His dad pointed to a gold key next to it. 'Open it and find out,' he said darkly.

With great curiosity, Orson opened the mystery box and discovered a gold pin resting upon a red velvet cushion. Inscribed on its lustrous surface were the words *'I believe in magic'.*

'I *was* the Grand Master,' said Martin Whitlock. 'So was your grandfather before me, but the contract states that if the Grand Master's health deteriorates to a point where he or she cannot perform their duties, then they must pass the title on. I've chosen you, Orson, to succeed me.'

Orson was speechless. 'But—'

His dad smiled. 'You're the new Grand Master with immediate effect. It's a very prestigious position. The title of Grand Master is the highest professional accolade that we have in magic.'

'But—' mumbled Orson.

'Don't worry,' said his dad. 'All you'll have to do is attend the official inauguration ceremony. That's about it to begin with. Until next Christmas.'

'Does Mum know about any of this?' asked Orson.

Orson's dad shook his head. 'No. Strict rules of confidentiality. I wasn't allowed to tell family members. Not even your mother.'

Orson couldn't believe his ears. To think that his dad had been keeping all of this a secret for so many years!

Martin Whitlock wheeled himself over to the photograph that his son had been so inquisitive about. He pointed to the young man in the photograph. 'His name is Daxton. A couple of years ago, he was expelled from the Society of Magicians. His stage name is Daxton the Destroyer.'

Orson sighed. 'Lovely name.'

Martin Whitlock laughed, then added, 'Yeah, well, as the name suggests, he's not a very charming man.'

'Why was he expelled from the Society of Magicians?' asked Orson.

Orson's dad threw his hands in the air. 'He kept breaking the magician's code.'

'You mean, he was selling secrets?' said Orson.

'To the highest bidder,' replied Martin Whitlock with a nod. 'It's strictly forbidden in the magic circle. You never reveal the secrets to tricks or illusions.' He shook his head. 'Never ever.'

Orson closed the mystery box, listening with the utmost attention to every word coming out of his father's mouth.

'No magician is above the laws of the society,' Orson's dad went on. 'Daxton had to go. But he's a vengeful character. If he ever becomes the Grand Master, he'll do untold damage to magic in this country.'

Orson sighed. 'That can't happen.'

His dad frowned. 'Expelling Daxton was a controversial decision. A sizeable cohort of people in the Society of Magicians swore allegiance to Daxton. A bitter rivalry ignited between both sides. Daxton has been trying to get his hands on this mystery box ever since.'

'Why?' asked Orson. 'What use is a gold pin to him?'

Martin Whitlock shook his head. 'Regrettably, there is a loophole. Whoever wears the gold pin, whether elected or not, can claim to be the Grand Master. No questions asked.'

'That's stupid,' cried Orson.

Orson's dad couldn't agree more. 'That's why I keep the mystery box locked under the floorboards, Orson. He'll never get to it. I've also given another mystery box to a friend of mine. An exact replica. This will throw Daxton off your scent. At least, for a while.'

Orson cringed. 'I met Daxton. He was in the library last week. He knew who I was.'

'I shouldn't worry, Orson,' said his father. 'He's not stupid. He wouldn't hurt you until he has got his greedy hands on the mystery box.'

This didn't make Orson feel much better. 'Oh, great.'

Orson's dad laughed.

'You said I have to attend an inauguration?' said Orson, raising his eyebrows.

'That's right.'

'What's that all about?'

'It's an event where you'll have to sign a document to make your appointment as Grand Master official,' explained his dad.

Orson grimaced. 'You said something about next Christmas, though, Dad?'

'My two-year term comes to an end,' replied Martin Whitlock. 'So next Christmas, your leadership of the Society of Magicians will be challenged by Daxton. He will compete against you and the winner will be the Grand Master for the next two years. You'll have to go up against him on stage, and whichever one of you performs the highest standard of magic, wins.'

Orson nearly dropped the mystery box. 'What?'

'I'm not saying it'll be easy, but look around you. Look at where you are! You can beat him, Orson, if you fully commit to it.'

Orson shook his head. 'What if I don't have what it takes?'

'Then we're all in terrible trouble,' replied Orson's dad.

Orson was speechless.

'Look, Daxton is performing at a venue in London tomorrow night,' said Martin Whitlock. 'I want you to go and watch him. See what you're up against.'

Orson stowed the mystery box back where he'd found it. 'Okay, I'll try my best.'

'That's all I'm asking,' said his dad.

Orson frowned for a moment. 'Do I have a good seat for tomorrow night?'

'What do you mean?'

'The ticket?' said Orson. 'Let me have a look. I'll check what row I'm in.'

'I don't have a ticket,' exclaimed Orson's dad.

Orson shrugged. 'Then how am I supposed to get in?'

'You're a magician,' replied his dad. 'Find a way in!'

'Fair enough,' said Orson. 'Can I bring someone with me?'

His dad was nodding. 'Of course you can. Who do you have in mind?'

CHAPTER THIRTEEN

The Greatest Magician of all Time

Orson and Agatha stood near the back of the queue, peering up at the huge theatre. The queues had begun to form since early evening and massive banners of 'Daxton the Destroyer' hung over the walls of the ancient building.

The banners depicted the famed magician posing with his arms folded and there was a very serious expression upon his face. The very same image adorned the many posters stuck on the nearby telephone boxes and electricity poles.

Orson averted his eyes and straightened his red tie. A little earlier, he had popped into the Centre of Excellence and borrowed one of the finest black suits he could possibly find in his size. He was well groomed as well, having slicked his hair back with some gel. He looked very dapper, as if he was performing in this evening's show himself.

'So, how do we get in without tickets?' asked Agatha, pushing up her glasses.

Orson frowned. 'Not sure yet,' he told her. 'I'll think of something. Or you will, hopefully.'

Agatha didn't dismiss the suggestion out of hand, which gave Orson some hope.

'Have you got an idea?' he asked her hopefully. 'You do, don't you?!'

Agatha smiled. 'I might.'

'Please tell me your mum works here?' said Orson.

Agatha shook her head. 'Wishful thinking. You can do card magic, right?'

Orson nodded. 'Of course.'

Agatha frowned. 'Anything else?'

'Anything else?' cried Orson indignantly. 'I can do lots of stuff. Money tricks, coin vanishes, sleight of hand, mind reading, levitations and much more, too. The list is endless.'

Agatha's eyes went wide behind her glasses. 'Did you say money?'

'Yes,' replied Orson.

'Get ready to do a money trick then,' Agatha told him.

There were many different entry points with queues every bit as long at each one. As expected, security was tight with ticket inspectors manning every single door.

Agatha looked at Orson. 'Pick a lady,' she told him.

Orson shrugged. 'Why?'

'Women are generally nicer than men,' replied Agatha. 'Especially to children. A woman is less likely to turn us away.'

Orson shrugged again, finding it hard to argue with Agatha's logic. 'Fair enough.'

They picked an entrance where a middle-aged lady was flashing a lovely smile at each person as she checked their ticket and sent them on their way into the theatre.

For such a long queue, it moved rather quickly and the closer Orson got to the door, the more nervous he became. His dad was testing him. If he returned home without gaining access to the show, then it would say a lot about his inability to manipulate people. Charisma was needed! He simply had to get in.

Waiting patiently, Orson wished he didn't have to listen to all the excited chatter around him, as people of all ages bided their time until it was their turn to enter the venue.

Two middle-aged men just in front of him in the queue were debating the greatest magicians of all time. He recognised some of the names mentioned from books he'd read in the library.

The two men mutually agreed that all of the magicians mentioned had undoubtedly left their mark on the craft, and that their names would be forever immortalised in the history books. But who was the best?

Some of the names cited were famous escapologists, while other performers were synonymous for their coin or card magic. Another magician, who was ranked highly by the men, was renowned for his mentalism abilities, and a few others did psychological tricks to confound the audience.

However, the conclusion agreed upon, whether due to their excitement at the impending live show, or perhaps not wishing to start an argument amongst his loyal supporters, was that 'Daxton the Destroyer' was the greatest magician and illusionist of all time. He could do it all and more.

The three ladies in the opposite queue said something similar, and one of them admitted that she was about to see him perform tonight for the fifth time in as many months.

'The greatest live show that I've ever been to,' she said to one of her excited friends.

Orson suddenly realised the enormity of the task before him. It would be no mean feat to beat Daxton.

However, all that would have to wait as he and Agatha were now positioned fourth and fifth, respectively, from the top of the queue. The people just ahead of them were being separated both left and right.

One person would go, ticket in hand, to the doorway where the middle-aged woman was manning the entry point, while another would hot-foot it to where the man was standing.

'If you're sent to the woman,' said Agatha, 'say you're lost and that your parents are inside.'

Orson laughed. 'Great idea!' He took another look at the man, whose very frame almost blocked the entrance. 'And what about him?'

'Money,' said Agatha quickly. 'He'll take a bribe.'

As Agatha headed off in the direction of the lady, Orson was selected to make his way towards the large man guarding the doorway. His stomach rumbled, but he mustered up the courage and turned towards the door. It was showtime! He eyed the man beckoning him to come forward.

Taking a deep breath, he did just that.

CHAPTER FOURTEEN

Daxton the Destroyer

'I can't let you in,' said the man gruffly. 'This is an all-ticket event. I'm sorry, but you can't pay at the door. The event has sold out.'

Orson smiled. 'What's your name, sir?'

'John.'

'I'm performing here tonight, John,' said Orson confidently.

John was taken aback. 'You are?'

'Yes,' said Orson. 'I'm a magician.'

Agatha had turned back upon seeing Orson's difficulties and rushed over. 'He *is* performing here tonight,' she said. 'Don't you know who he is?'

John took a prolonged look at Orson. 'Well, he's a kid! I know that much.'

'You've never heard of "Orson the Great"?' cried Agatha, waving her hands animatedly in the air.

John looked none the wiser. 'Can't say that I have.'

'Well, you will,' replied Agatha. 'He's going to be the greatest magician in the world someday.'

'Tell you what, "Orson the Great",' said John. 'You do something magical and I'll let you in for free!'

Orson removed a single slip of blank white paper, about the size of a cheque, from his inner jacket pocket and showed it to John. 'No, I'll pay,' he said, producing a box of matches from his trouser pocket.

John shot Orson a worried look. 'You're not going to burn the theatre down, are you?'

'I was just about to ask,' said Orson. 'Is the building insured for fire damage?'

John laughed nervously. 'Well, I hope that was a joke!'

From the matchbox, Orson took out a single match and then crumpled the slip of paper into a ball, before holding it out.

'John, I need your help,' he said.

'Okay,' said John. 'What do you want me to do?'

Orson handed John the matchbox and the match. 'When I tell you to, I want you to light the paper in my hand.'

Orson held the crumpled ball of paper in the air with both hands. 'John,' he said in a serious voice.

John was smiling like a kid at his own birthday party. 'What?'

'Light the paper!'

John struck the match. 'You're sure?!'

'Do it now!' cried Orson, looking at the diminishing flame.

John lit the paper with the head of the match and it ignited into a small flame.

When the flame had subsided, Orson slowly uncrumpled the paper in his hand to reveal that, incredibly, it had transformed into a fifty pound note. He handed the money to John. 'Merry Christmas!'

A round of applause went up, courtesy of the half a dozen girls who'd been watching the magic unfolding with interest in the queue.

John burst out laughing and held the fifty pound note up, looking for any signs of singe marks. It was perfect. He scratched his head. 'Well, there you go! You're "Orson the Great" after all.' He moved to one side. 'Enjoy the show, Orson!'

Orson smiled, thanked him and walked inside.

'Your boyfriend is very talented,' said John to Agatha as she walked past him.

'He's not my boyfriend!' exclaimed Agatha in horror. She caught up with Orson. 'Did you hear that?'

Orson laughed. 'Yeah, I heard.'

They continued along a wide corridor, lit only by floor lights, and were soon in a busy foyer, where excited people of all ages were gathered. It was twenty minutes before curtains were up and there was a palpable sense of excitement in the air.

Everywhere he looked, Orson saw people with magic wands in their hands and top hats on their heads. Accompanied with black capes and white gloves, they all looked suitably dressed for the occasion.

He was conflicted. To see so many people here in admiration of a man whom he hoped to emulate and, indeed, compete against this time next year should have been agony for him.

And yet, despite all this, he was excited to be here and to get the chance to see Daxton in action. It was a magic show, after all! And he loved magic.

People were looking from the tickets in their hands to the numbers above the doorways, trying to figure out where exactly they had to enter the theatre.

Although Orson and Agatha had no such concerns, it was time to get a move on if they wanted to find two free seats. Given the crowd, Orson knew that they might be forced to go up to the higher galleries in the hope of finding a couple of vacant seats.

'Sorry,' said Orson, almost getting in the way of three children who were carrying large bags of popcorn and bottles of soft drinks into the theatre.

Agatha bought a programme and handed it to Orson. 'You hold that,' she said, then pointed over to one of the many snack bars in the foyer. 'Want any popcorn?'

Although the smell of popcorn was quite enticing, and had this been a normal trip to, say, the cinema, then Orson would've undoubtedly accepted Agatha's kind offer. However, this show felt a little too serious to be sitting back and munching on goodies. He had to study Daxton's every move and look for flaws. 'No,' he replied.

'Suit yourself,' said Agatha. 'I'm getting some.'

As Agatha crossed the foyer, Orson looked around. He was in the lower tier of the theatre and he caught sight of what he presumed were crew members of the magic show mingling with the crowd.

The crew members were kind enough to allow some fans to take photographs with them, before they headed off through a side door to get ready for the show.

As he waited for Agatha, Orson flicked through the programme and read some of the endorsements of the show from newspapers, magazines and other renowned publications from around the world.

The headlines jumped out at him.

'YOU WILL BE UNDER DAXTON THE DESTROYER'S SPELL.'

'GROUNDBREAKING.'

'STUNNING AND FLAWLESS.'

'A POWERHOUSE.'

'A KNOCKOUT.'

He sighed before reading the next one. 'The multi-award-winning master of magic and mind control returns to London for a one-off performance.' There were many more accolades listed, but Orson closed the programme. He could read no more.

Agatha came walking over to him carrying a large bag of fluffy popcorn and a medium-sized coke, with the bag of sweets she'd also purchased tucked securely in her jacket pocket.

'You're sure you don't want some popcorn?' she asked him.

'Sweet or salted?' asked Orson.

'Salted,' replied Agatha. 'Always.'

Orson suddenly realised that the teenaged boy behind the counter, whose name tag identified him as Jake, was holding out a soft drink in one hand and beckoning Agatha back with the other.

'Your coke!' cried Jake.

Agatha turned and sighed, before rushing back over to the snack bar.

'You almost forgot your boyfriend's coke,' said Jake with a smile, handing the coke over.

Rolling her eyes, Agatha replied, 'He's not my boyfriend!'

'Whatever you say,' said Jake with a knowing smile.

Agatha carried the coke back over to Orson, who'd changed his mind regarding the popcorn and scooped a handful from the top of the pile.

As they entered the theatre through a pair of double doors, Orson realised that they were in the stalls, the section closest to the stage. He turned to Agatha. 'So, where should we start looking? There must be a couple of spare seats around here somewhere.'

'Um, go—' Agatha's reply was cut short by a booming voice that reverberated around the theatre.

'Please take your seats. The performance will begin in ten minutes.'

Anticipation was building as audience members found their seats.

'C'mon, let's head up to the top rows,' said Agatha, pointing a finger upwards. 'I think I see a few seats up at the back.'

Orson sighed. 'They're probably reserved.'

'Well, we can sit in them until someone arrives,' replied Agatha doggedly.

Agatha began to ascend the steps, but Orson had turned right around and was looking back at the stage.

'What is it?' asked Agatha.

'Nothing,' said Orson. 'Yeah, good idea. You go up to those seats. I'll be up in a minute.' With his coke in one hand, he rushed down the steps and left the theatre by the door through which he had entered.

The foyer was still reasonably busy, with people rushing to buy drinks from the bar and treats from the shop before the start of the show.

Jake was sweeping the popcorn and crisps off the floor when Orson walked past him and made his way over to the stage door. He put his coke down on a ledge and saw a sign that read 'NO STAFF BEYOND THIS POINT'. He tried to open the door, but it was locked.

Pulling a paperclip from his pocket, Orson was about to embark on an attempt to pick the lock, when he heard voices on the other side of the door. The stroke of luck he needed!

When the door swung open and three security men came walking out, he hid in the shadows and stopped the door from closing with his hand. He was in!

The path before him was dark and where precisely it led, he did not know, but onwards he walked towards a light at the end of the corridor. When he got near the end, he realised that, rather than being backstage, he was actually at the side of the stage.

The first thing that Orson noticed was that the stage was deserted. Then the curtains began to part very slowly and there were uproarious cheers from the audience. He scanned the stage. As far as he could tell, there was still no Daxton. Where was he?

Without any notable sign of 'The Destroyer', Orson felt like walking out onto the stage himself and accepting the round of applause before jumping straight into one of his 'go-to' tricks.

What a bold statement that would be! Sabotaging a competitor's show that was being watched by hundreds of people.

He allowed himself a moment to daydream. What trick would he do for an opener? Something visual like a coin jump? Or perhaps something more dramatic like a mentalism effect?

Regardless of the choice of magic, the audacious stunt would make headlines around the world and would give him instant stardom. It was an impulse he might've acted upon had it not been for Daxton's sudden appearance on stage.

Whether Daxton was lowered by wires, or perhaps emerged through a trap door system, Orson couldn't say for sure. But somehow, 'The Destroyer' was now standing in the middle of the stage and he was the picture of serenity and focus.

There was a massive screen behind the stage for close-up shots. Apart from that, Daxton wasn't accompanied by an orchestra or any musicians and there were no props of any description, at least none that Orson could see.

Daxton did cut a dapper figure, though, dressed in a black suit with a white shirt, which was unbuttoned to the chest.

He stood there calmly, awaiting the curtains to fully open. When they did, he took a deep breath and raised his arms out wide.

CHAPTER FIFTEEN

A Master at Work

Orson couldn't believe his eyes. Daxton was like a different person. He turned on the charm, wishing everyone a belated Merry Christmas, and spoke about his hopes that the new year ahead would be a prosperous one for everyone present.

As he stood in the shadows, Orson moved a little closer, his eyes fixed upon Daxton.

'Hands up if the twenty-eighth of December is your birthday?' asked Daxton, who raised his own hand into the air.

Orson took a few paces to his right, trying to angle a better look at the audience.

Daxton laughed heartily when a few hands in the theatre rose high into the air. 'I feel your pain,' he said sympathetically. 'I used to get presents on Christmas morning and my birthday was simply overlooked! It's not so bad now, but try telling a nine-year-old kid that he's not getting a birthday cake.'

The entire house gave a unified, 'Aww!'

Daxton invited one of the birthday contingent up on stage. She was a little girl who was seated in the third row from the front.

'Is it really your birthday?' asked Daxton when the girl had got up on stage.

'Yep,' replied the girl excitedly. 'I'm nine.'

As Daxton escorted the girl across the stage and discovered that her name was Orla, a few attendants wheeled onto the stage a gigantic box wrapped in crimson and gold paper.

'Wow,' said Orla. 'Is that for me?'

Daxton laughed hysterically. 'Did you get everything you asked for at Christmas?'

'I did,' replied Orla, eyes on the box.

Daxton said, 'Well, I've a present for you. But before you open it, I want you to know one thing.'

Orla nodded. 'Can I open it?!'

The crowd laughed out loud.

'You've a few *hurdles* to jump over first,' replied Daxton with a chuckle. 'Now, you can have anything you want.'

Orla's eyes widened. 'Anything?'

Daxton gently took hold of Orla's wrist. 'It would be quite easy for you to take the *reins* and say the first thing that comes into your head, like a space rocket or something like that, given we've been *rocking* up to the moon of late. But *horse* around for a bit and think about it. It's not a *gallop*. Take your time.'

The girl looked in deep thought. 'I know,' she said after a moment.

'You're sure?' asked Daxton. 'Take your time. It's a free choice.'

Orla was adamant. 'No, I'm sure.'

'Tell us,' said Daxton.

'A rocking horse!' said the girl.

'A rocking horse,' repeated Daxton, looking amused by the choice. 'Interesting. You'd better open the present and find out.'

With a smile, Orla tried to push the lid of the box open, but in the end she needed some assistance from one of the stagehands. The lid fell open a moment later and inside, incredibly, was a toy rocking horse.

As Orla jumped onto the horse, the crowd applauded and cheered.

Daxton bowed.

'Can I keep it?' asked Orla.

'A promise is a promise, Orla,' said Daxton. 'It's all yours. Can I just ask you one more question, if you don't mind, before I send you back to your mum?'

Orla jumped off the horse.

'Don't say it out loud,' resumed Daxton, 'but I want you to think about your favourite present on Christmas morning.'

Orla nodded. 'Can I tell you?'

'No, don't say it!' said Daxton, laughing as he looked into Orla's eyes. 'Just think the answer.'

Orla nodded.

'We're heading back to space again, aren't we?' exclaimed Daxton a moment later. 'It's a space hopper. Am I right? Is it a space hopper?'

A smile spread across Orla's face. 'Yeah.'

The audience began to applaud as Daxton gave Orla a hug before sending her back into the audience, where she took up her seat next to her mum.

Pacing around the stage, Daxton looked troubled. 'Well, of course I know what you're all thinking. That was easy. Every kid in the country got a space hopper for Christmas this year.' He looked at Orla's mum in the third row. 'Mum, would you mind coming up on stage?'

Orla's mum sat up straight and seemed a little reluctant, but the round of applause soon gave her the necessary encouragement that she needed to leave her seat.

'Lovely to meet you,' said Daxton, shaking the woman's hand when she had climbed the steps and had made her way up on stage. 'How are you?'

Orla's mum replied with a frown, 'Nervous.'

'Don't be nervous,' said Daxton. 'What's your name?'

'Jessica.'

Daxton smiled. 'I'm just going to try to extract a word from your mind,' said Daxton. 'Could you think of a word, please? A completely random word, and you can change your mind as many times as you like before settling on one.'

Jessica mused over this for a moment.

'Got one?' asked Daxton.

'Yes,' answered Jessica.

'Think of that word,' said Daxton, looking into her eyes. 'Just say the word in your mind. Not out loud, but just think it. Say it repeatedly in your mind, please.'

Daxton looked into Jessica's eyes and said after a moment, 'I'm going to go with "umbrella". Is it an umbrella you're thinking of?'

The lady nodded with a beaming smile. 'Yes, you're right.'

Talking over the sustained applause, Daxton said, 'Oh, I meant to say, did you break your arm recently? I'll be more specific. Your right wrist?'

'Yes,' replied Jessica, clasping her right hand. 'I had to wear a cast for two months.'

Daxton nodded. 'I can tell by your posture,' he told her.

Jessica raised her eyebrows. 'Really?'

'You walk as if the cast is still there,' said Daxton. 'You slipped and fell in the park when you went for a walk. At first, you thought it was just your right leg that was injured, but over the next couple of days your wrist began to hurt, so you went to your local hospital and had an x-ray.'

Jessica held a hand over her mouth, stunned. 'There's no way you could know that.'

'And, by the way you're dressed,' continued Daxton, 'I think I can tell what you do for a living.' He took a backward step and looked down at her shoes. 'Something tells me you're in healthcare. A health provider of some form or another. Am I on the right lines?'

Jessica nodded and laughed.

'Not a nurse,' said Daxton, 'but more in the recovery end of things.'

There was another nod by Jessica, before Daxton added, 'You're a physiotherapist. Is that it?'

Jessica had had enough. She threw her arms into the air, amazed. 'Yes!'

Daxton heaved a heavy sigh. 'You're a little troubled about a big change in your life, as well. Something you feel sentimental about. Would you mind showing me your hands for a moment?'

Doing as she was instructed, Jessica held her hands up.

'You're moving house,' exclaimed Daxton after a moment. 'Is that it?'

'The removal van arrived this morning!' replied Jessica, trying not to blush.

Daxton smiled kindly. 'Well, I wish you and your family the very best of luck with your new move.'

Orson watched all this in awe. Daxton's routine was stunning and his considerable stagecraft and presence was a sight to behold.

Even from his vantage point at the side of the stage, Orson found himself being fooled by more tricks than he'd like to admit.

From his reading of mentalism books, Orson knew that Daxton used a variety of techniques to acquire information from people without their knowledge.

This could include cold reading, suggestion techniques and subliminal messages to influence the responses of the spectators.

In some cases, it could be something as simple as educated guesswork that was involved – predictions based on similar memories experienced by the majority of people. For the rest of the first half of the show, Orson treated it like a checklist.

Every time Daxton performed an illusion, whether it was a close-up card trick, or teleporting a spectator's signed ten pound note to the inside of a lemon, Orson tried to figure out the method. He had to be quick, as Daxton went seamlessly from one routine to another in a relentless fashion, displaying his full repertoire of skills.

There was a dangerous bullet catch, a floating lightbulb effect, a baffling prediction involving random numbers freely chosen by five subjects. Then he performed what he told the audience was his signature trick – levitating from the stage to end the first half, after which the giant red curtains closed.

Orson was in a daze. By any standards, Daxton was a master. His magic was compelling and some of the illusions he pulled off were the stuff of fantasy. In short, the first half performance by Daxton had been a stunning masterclass in magic.

Orson knew he had a lot of catching up to do if he was going to get anywhere near Daxton's level, let alone defeat him. He was about to leave the side of the stage and make his way back out, when he suddenly heard Daxton shouting at someone.

Turning around again, Orson saw a young boy of about fourteen standing before Daxton with his head hung.

On the other side of the curtains, the musical interlude had started up, so obviously the celebrated magician felt confident enough to raise his voice to such a loud level.

From what Orson could gather, the reprimand seemed to centre on the slow removal of a prop around the midway point of the first half. The charming façade that Daxton had displayed for the last hour or so had finally slipped.

Orson watched this unpleasant incident with interest until the boy fled the stage, on the verge of tears. If he didn't leave now, Orson knew that Daxton would eventually turn around and spot him.

'The Destroyer' wiped beads of perspiration from his brow and took a moment to compose himself.

Orson decided that he was going nowhere and waited for Daxton to see him.

When Daxton turned around and their eyes eventually met, Orson stared back with intent.

Daxton advanced menacingly towards him.

Orson stood his ground.

CHAPTER SIXTEEN

Gaining the Advantage

Daxton forced a smile. 'I told you, Orson, didn't I? I knew you'd want to speak to me the next time you saw me, and here we are.'

'Here we are,' said Orson. 'You've a lovely manner with your employees. They must love working for you.'

There was a tense silence.

Daxton narrowed his eyes. 'Oh, you mean Raymond just now. He can handle it. The price I pay for being a perfectionist. You've to step on a few toes from time to time. One day, you'll understand.'

Orson began to applaud. 'Great first half.'

'The second half is better,' replied Daxton. 'And, as for the finale, well, what can I say? Always finish strongly and leave the audience wanting more. I'm sure you've been told that.'

'One problem, though,' said Orson.

Daxton shook his head. 'What would that be?'

'The levitation act,' said Orson with a smile. 'I could see the wires.'

'I don't use wires,' replied Daxton peevishly.

'You're sure about that?' said Orson, his smile widening.

Daxton smiled back. 'Aw, what a shame.'

'What's a shame?' said Orson with a shake of his head.

'I thought you were a believer,' said Daxton. 'I didn't use wires.'

Orson laughed. 'Then how did you do it? How did you fly like that?'

'Never reveal a secret,' said Daxton. 'Surely you've learnt that by now?!'

'Bit rich coming from you,' replied Orson. 'Isn't that why you were thrown out of the Society of Magicians?'

A smile formed on Daxton's face. 'Is that what your father told you?! That's interesting. I've been reliably informed that *you* will be representing the Whitlock family next Christmas.'

'That's right,' said Orson.

'I had hoped,' said Daxton, 'for the sake of magic, that you would simply step aside and allow me to run unchallenged for the position of Grand Master. Do you intend to challenge me?'

'Of course I do,' said Orson determinedly.

Daxton replied, 'Your family have held the position of Grand Master for far too long.'

Orson shrugged. 'You want to be Grand Master that badly?'

Daxton glared at Orson.

'Why wait until next Christmas?' asked Orson.

'Pardon me?' said Daxton.

Orson took out of his pocket the gold pin and smiled. He pinned it to his jacket. 'Remember who you are talking to,' he said sharply. 'I *am* the Grand Master.'

'So you are,' said Daxton. 'For now.'

Orson shrugged. 'Come and take the pin off me. You'll never have a better chance. You're so close to your dream.'

With a frown, Daxton shook his head. 'You'd love nothing more than for me to stick a fake pin on my jacket and start telling my followers that I'm the new Grand Master.'

'It's not a fake,' said Orson. 'I promise.'

Daxton's frown formed into a smile. 'You overemphasised your lie with a subconscious tilt of your head and by raising your eyebrows. Both indicators of deception. You're lying!'

Orson looked emotionless. 'I'm not.'

'I'm in no rush,' said Daxton. 'I've waited all my life for this chance. I can wait one more year.'

Orson scowled at him. 'I think we're finished here. See you next Christmas.'

Daxton straightened his jacket and shot Orson a sinister look. 'I'll need to speak to you before then, but don't worry. I'll find you.'

Orson watched Daxton exit the stage. *I'll find you!* he thought to himself. What did Daxton mean by that? Was it a veiled threat?

When Daxton had left, Orson seized his opportunity and walked out into the middle of the deserted stage. Imagining the spotlight was upon him, he raised his hands into the air.

This was his stage. It was where he belonged. If tonight had taught him anything, it was this – he wanted to be like Daxton. No, it was more than that – he wanted to be *better* than Daxton. And he would be.

If he had to practise every moment of every single day between now and next Christmas Eve, then he would! If that's what it took to defeat this man, then he'd gladly do it.

Just then, a booming voice declared that it was five minutes until the commencement of the second half.

Orson had seen enough. He was leaving and so, too, was Agatha. If he could find her. He left the stage and quickly returned to the stalls in an effort to locate her.

As it turned out, Agatha found him, and dragged him over to a vacant seat right in the corner of the theatre.

'Where've you been?' asked Agatha crossly. 'I sat here by myself for the entire first half.'

'I had to do something,' said Orson. 'C'mon, we're leaving.'

Agatha was stunned. 'Leaving? I want to see the second half. Gosh, he's brilliant, isn't he, Orson? Incredible. Did you see him levitating at the end of the first half? I couldn't see any wires, either. How'd he do it?'

Orson rolled his eyes. 'He's all right,' he said curtly. 'Bit show offish. You know, over-the-top stuff.'

Agatha frowned. 'I'm sorry, Orson,' she said apologetically. 'This must be very hard for you watching him on stage like that and everyone roaring and shouting.'

Orson shot Agatha a sour look.

Agatha grabbed her coat. 'Okay, we'll go.'

No sooner had they pushed through the exit doors than they heard the cheers starting once more from inside the theatre. 'Daxton the Destroyer' was obviously back on the stage.

Jake was standing in the snack bar, busily counting coins from the till. He raised his eyes and saw a glum-looking Orson walking out with Agatha. He smiled and nodded at Orson. 'Leaving early? Date not going so well, huh?'

This comment made Orson break into a smile. However, when he looked across at Agatha she was stone faced.

Walking down a flight of stairs, Agatha noticed the gold pin sparkling on Orson's jacket. 'That's pretty,' she said. 'Is it real gold?'

Orson removed the pin and threw it in a nearby rubbish bin. 'It's a fake,' he grumbled.

When they got to the lower lobby, they sat down next to a life-size poster of Daxton and listened to the cheers above their heads that seemed to shake the very foundations of the building.

Orson, looking a little subdued, turned to Agatha. 'D'you think I can beat this man?'

'It'll be tough,' replied Agatha, pushing her glasses up. 'No point lying to you, but I believe anything is possible if you put your mind to it.'

Orson rested his chin on his hands. 'Yeah.'

'But he has the advantage at the moment,' said Agatha earnestly.

Orson stood up. 'What if I told you that there was a way for *me* to gain the advantage,' he said passionately.

'And how would you do that?' asked Agatha, intrigued.

CHAPTER SEVENTEEN

The Theatre

The following day, Agatha stood inside the Centre of Excellence and looked inquisitively around. By the glint in her eye, Orson could tell that she was impressed. How could she be anything otherwise?

'Amazing, isn't it?' said Orson with pride.

'It is,' said Agatha.

'There were weaknesses in Daxton's performance,' Orson told her.

Agatha grimaced. 'Really?' she said sceptically.

'Well, he had no large-scale effects,' said Orson, looking very serious. 'He also had no assistant. His ego is too big to share the stage with another person. He had no music. No orchestra. His show was very clichéd.'

Agatha smiled. 'Clichéd?

Orson smiled back. 'It means unoriginal.'

'I know what it means,' said Agatha indignantly. 'Where'd you learn that word?'

'The dictionary,' replied Orson.

'It's a good word,' said Agatha.

Orson laughed. 'My point is, Daxton's show had no razzamatazz.'

Agatha nodded. 'I see your point. So your show will have razzamatazz?'

'In bucket loads!' cried Orson.

Agatha was walking around, her eager eyes studying the array of books in the library. 'Any books on marketing?'

Orson wasn't listening. He was pacing the Centre of Excellence pensively. 'I want you to be my assistant.'

'Your assistant?' said Agatha, sounding indifferent. 'In what way? Make your tea and carry your coat!'

Orson waved his hands in the air. 'No! Nothing like that. I don't even like tea all that much!'

'Good,' said Agatha. 'Because I'm not mad on tea, either.'

Orson led Agatha around the Centre of Excellence and pointed to a large, rectangular box consisting of two separate parts. 'That's the kind of thing I'm talking about. I could saw you in half.'

Agatha gave Orson a bewildered look. 'Huh?'

Orson said, after a loud laugh, 'I don't actually saw you in half! I'm just making the point that, with your help, I'll be able to do different tricks. Bring something new to my performance. What d'you reckon?'

'I'll do it,' said Agatha after a moment. 'As long as I get full control over planning and preparation. That way, you'll be able to concentrate on your magic and performance.'

Orson was quite happy to accept this arrangement, as was his dad, who suddenly appeared at the top of the balcony on crutches, looking down at the two of them.

'Welcome to our team, young lady,' he said, his voice echoing.

'Dad, are you coming down?' Orson called out.

Martin Whitlock chuckled. 'If I can make it down!' Instead of using the ladder, he took the lift. When he made it to the bottom, he said, 'Forgive me, I wasn't eavesdropping, Orson. I was coming down to show you something and I was surprised to hear voices.'

'This is Agatha,' said Orson, intimating to Agatha with his hand.

Agatha smiled and pushed up her glasses. 'Nice to meet you, Mr Whitlock.'

'Oh, call me Martin,' replied Orson's dad, hobbling over to shake Agatha's hand. 'Lovely to meet you. I came down here to show Orson something. It concerns you now, too, Agatha.'

'Oh, really?' said Agatha, taken by surprise.

'Yes,' replied Martin Whitlock. Outstretching a crutch, he pointed to a bunch of keys hanging above a magical apparatus of some description that Orson hadn't gotten around to examining yet. 'I was down here a little earlier trying to get things ready for the big reveal.'

'What big reveal?' asked Orson.

His father was smiling and began hopping across the workshop on his crutches. 'There's one last secret in here, Orson,' he said mysteriously. 'I wanted to show you this myself. Take the keys and follow me.'

Orson grabbed the set of keys and followed his father over to a door at the back of the Centre of Excellence. Unlocking it, he helped his dad inside and flicked on the lights.

'Oh, wow,' said Agatha, who had followed them.

Orson's eyes twinkled. He was looking out at a small theatre that was able to hold maybe one hundred people by his estimates. There were luxury padded seats that had ample leg room and a cupholder on the armrest for a spectator's soft drink.

The stage itself was of a decent size and the red curtains surrounding it were drawn back, as if a magician's entrance was imminent.

There was even a snack bar with the traditional stand of freshly made popcorn and a soft-drinks dispenser. Hung behind the counter were bags of chocolate treats and packets of crisps. It was a lovely little theatre. Quaint and old-fashioned perhaps, but lovely, nonetheless.

'No point being the Grand Master of the Society of Magicians,' said Martin Whitlock, 'and having nowhere to practise your routines.'

Orson was astounded.

Orson's dad smiled at him. 'I honed my craft in this theatre. So did your grandfather. There were many long, solitary hours spent in here practising my routines. Reaching the top requires a lot of self-sacrifice. This is hallowed ground for our family. You can—'

Orson threw his arms around his dad's waist. 'It's amazing. Thanks, Dad.'

His father laughed. 'I was just going to say that you can fulfil your potential here. Daxton won't know what's hit him next Christmas, will he, Orson?'

Orson sighed. 'I'm going to give it my best shot.'

'That's the spirit,' said Orson's dad with enthusiasm. 'Now, your inauguration ceremony is in Edinburgh on New Year's Day. You'll have to travel there and sign a document to make your appointment official.'

Orson was suddenly very excited. He'd never been to Scotland.

'I've never been to Scotland,' said Agatha.

'Can you come with me?' asked Orson, looking at her.

Agatha smiled. 'I'll have to ask my mum and dad, obviously. How are we going to get there?'

Orson shook his head and looked up at his dad enquiringly.

'Oh,' said Martin Whitlock. 'I've all that arranged.'

'It would be a lovely journey on the train,' said Orson with a smile.

His father nodded. 'You're going on the train, yes. Your uncle is travelling with you as well.'

Orson's eyes lit up. 'Brian's coming for New Years? That's brilliant. Haven't seen him in an age.'

'Uncle Tom,' said Orson's dad.

Orson hesitated. 'Uncle Tom? Is that a good idea, Dad? Tom doesn't know about the family secret, does he?'

'No, he certainly doesn't, Orson,' replied his dad. 'But I don't want you travelling by yourself on the train. Tom thinks he's taking you to the dentist. Look, Orson, I'd drive you myself, but obviously I can't.'

Orson was far from thrilled with this arrangement, but what else could he do? Unless he aged several years, passed his driving test and bought himself a shiny new car in the next couple of days, then he was heading with his Uncle Tom to Edinburgh on New Year's Day, whether he liked it or not.

So, too, was Agatha, who phoned the Whitlocks on the morning of New Year's Eve and confirmed her attendance at the ceremony.

*

In keeping with tradition, Orson's grandparents arrived later in the evening and they all bid farewell to the old year and offered blessings to the new one by linking hands and swaying to 'Auld Lang Syne'.

Orson found all this very embarrassing and he was thankful that his assistant, Agatha, wasn't around to see any of it.

When the countdown to the new year was over, everyone retired to their rooms.

Orson's mum planted a kiss on his forehead. 'Happy New Year, Orson. May all your dreams come true. See you in the morning, before you leave.'

'Night, Mum,' said Orson.

On his way up the stairs, Francis L. Whitlock stopped to wish his grandson the best of luck for tomorrow evening's ceremony. 'Feels like only yesterday when I was heading over to Dublin for my New Year's Day inauguration.'

'Your inauguration ceremony was in Dublin?' asked Orson.

Orson's grandfather nodded. 'Indeed it was, young man. The location of the inauguration changes every time a new Grand Master is appointed, to maintain its secrecy. I wasn't as young as you are, though. You'll be the youngest ever Grand Master. It's great fun, Orson, enjoy the day!'

'Thanks, Grandad.'

Orson could hear his dad's crutches clacking on the floorboards.

'Goodnight, Dad,' said Martin Whitlock, watching his father ascend the stairs, before turning around to his son. 'Orson, I've left the mystery box on your bed. You mustn't forget that!'

'I won't,' replied Orson. Then he hugged his dad.

'Good luck tomorrow,' said his dad with tears in his eyes.

'Thanks, Dad,' replied Orson. He then climbed the stairs, went into his room and opened the mystery box. He smiled when he saw the gold pin resting upon the red cushion, but he didn't touch it and closed the lid.

What should he do now? He wasn't one bit tired.

Instead of going to sleep, Orson got changed into his tuxedo and waited until the house was quiet, before he tiptoed down the stairs and made his way into the Centre of Excellence. The door to the theatre was still ajar from a couple of days ago and he stepped inside.

At night, with the lights dimmed, the theatre looked magical, mystical even. Orson switched on the stage lights, but kept the seating area dark, as if he were about to perform to a full house.

And so, in the early hours of the year 1972, Orson performed trick after trick, over and over again. In his imagination, he spoke to the audience and they answered him back.

A chosen spectator stood by his side and she marvelled as he told her about one of her fondest childhood memories, of which he could not possibly have known. He listened to his adoring fans cheer, laugh and call out 'Orson the Great' in unison.

And, when the triumphant performance came to an end, he stood in the middle of the stage and luxuriated in the standing ovation. He held his arms out wide. He was born to do this. Of course he was! He was 'Orson the Great', after all.

CHAPTER EIGHTEEN

Edinburgh

After a hearty breakfast early the next morning, Orson left with his Uncle Tom and, of course, his assistant Agatha, whom they collected on the way to the train station.

They arrived at King's Cross station about an hour before departure and sat around the platform drinking cups of coffee to while away the time. When it was time to board, they managed to find a carriage together and stored their suitcases in the overhead compartments.

It was a long journey, which Orson broke up with regular naps and a three-course dinner. He also read his book on suggestion, body language and behavioural psychology. He'd taken it from the library in the Centre of Excellence and it was very interesting.

Every time he saw somebody now, whether they were simply walking down the street or shopping in a supermarket, he tried to guess what they did for a living. Just by the way they walked, or even the clothes they wore, he could hazard an educated guess.

Of course, running up to random people and asking them what they actually *did* do for a living could be a little awkward, but he had no choice. He had to master all this if he was going to add another element of magic to his routine.

His uncle, meanwhile, took a snooze, which afforded Orson and Agatha a chance to talk about the upcoming schedule for the day. They had the hotel name and the address, and they knew the conference room number where the ceremony was taking place. The start time of eight o'clock was duly noted.

'We're also going to do some sightseeing,' said Agatha, flicking through a brochure on Edinburgh that was sitting on the table in the carriage.

Orson smiled. 'Really?'

'We have time,' Agatha assured him.

Uncle Tom was dozing in and out of sleep. 'Sightseeing?' he said with a yawn, stretching himself.

'What d'you reckon, Tom?' said Orson, looking up from his book. 'Fancy some sightseeing while you're in Edinburgh?'

Tom grimaced. 'Gosh, I'd love to, Orson, I really would. But there's a documentary on business and the evolution in technology on television tonight.'

Orson shook his head and frowned.

Agatha sat up, her interest piqued. 'Is there?'

Tom was folding the newspaper, trying to locate the television listings. 'What channel is it on? I wouldn't like to miss it. I might just stay in my room to watch that.'

'Is that the area you work in, Tom?' asked Agatha.

Tom smiled. 'It is indeed, Agatha.'

'What do you do?' asked Agatha curiously.

Tom hesitated. 'Uh, err, I'm an accountant,' he stuttered.

'Oh, that's an interesting job,' said Agatha. 'I like numbers, too. Marketing as well.'

'Oh, brilliant,' exclaimed Tom. 'Our company has a marketing department that you'd be perfect for someday.'

'I'm fascinated by communications as well,' added Agatha. 'How we communicate with each other, and what the future advances will be within the area with the emergence of computers.'

As Orson sat listening to this conversation, he couldn't help noticing the body language of his uncle. If he didn't know any better, he might've thought that his mum's brother was lying at times.

For example, when Agatha asked him what he did for a living, his uncle hesitated and seemed uncomfortable for a moment, as if he'd forgotten what it was he actually did. It wasn't like him.

Furthermore, when Tom took a moment to respond, he looked up to his right to remember his current job. According to the book Orson was currently reading, these were all tell-tale signs of a lie. Although it wasn't always foolproof by any means, it was a fairly good indicator of deceit.

Of course, Orson knew he was over analysing everybody more and more these days. His poor uncle had just woken up.

Orson had devoured so many books lately on mentalism, lie detection and psychology, that he could hardly talk to a person without trying to guess things about them.

'We've a fax machine now,' said Tom.

Orson tried not to smile. No mind reading was required. His uncle was definitely telling the truth this time.

Agatha looked genuinely interested. 'Gosh, I've never even seen a fax machine.'

'Ah, they're amazing,' replied Tom. 'They're the future. Every office will soon have one. Great fun, too. So many hilarious stories about them already. Isn't that right, Orson?'

Orson buried his head in his book. 'Yep,' he said sheepishly.

As Uncle Tom regaled Agatha with the exciting work incident involving the fax machine, Orson returned to his reading.

The train sped on and, by two o'clock in the afternoon, they had arrived in Edinburgh, where they got a taxi to their hotel. After checking in, they all did their own thing.

Uncle Tom slipped into his flip-flops and made the short journey from his room to the hotel's pool. Agatha looked around the shops in the lobby, and Orson went in search of the conference room where he would later be sworn in as Grand Master.

When he found it, he saw a sign outside the doors stating that the conference room was reserved for a 'sales meeting' that was taking place at eight o'clock that evening. This was definitely the room then!

Walking in, he saw perhaps a hundred chairs set out before a stage. There was also an area reserved for tea and coffee with trays of sandwiches, biscuits and cakes already spread out on the tableclothed tables.

Orson walked over and picked up a chocolate biscuit. He was about to become the youngest ever Grand Master of the Society of Magicians. Surely, that gave him special authorisation to sample the first biscuit. He was just about to take a bite of the biscuit, when a man dressed in a fine black suit came strolling into the conference room.

'Who are you?' asked the man.

'Orson.'

'Whitlock?' asked the man, raising his eyebrows.

Orson smiled. 'Yes.'

'Well, it's lovely to meet you,' said the man, offering his hand. 'I must say, I wasn't expecting the Grand Master to be here so early. I'm Magnus.'

Orson shook Magnus' hand. 'Nice to meet you.'

Magnus was about forty-five. However, an older man now presented himself in the conference room and he was looking quite confused. He was also dressed in a black suit, but his tie was crooked and his shirt tail was hanging out.

'Ah, Orson, I'd like you to meet my father, Bernard,' said Magnus.

'Who are you?' asked Bernard, peering down at Orson.

Magnus smiled. 'This is Orson.'

'Is he here for his revelation?' the father asked the son.

Magnus turned pale and stared at his father.

'What does that mean?' asked Orson.

Magnus shook his head. 'Dad's thinking of something else. Sorry, Orson.'

Orson then noticed Magnus mouthing the words 'Be quiet!' to his father.

Orson sensed something was up with this father and son duo, and he didn't need to consult his book on body language to confirm his suspicions. A person plucked from the street with zero knowledge of body language would be able to read the tell-tale signs, never mind a magician like himself.

Magnus shook his head. 'Dad, Orson is here for his inauguration. Tonight, he'll be officially declared as the Grand Master of the Society of Magicians.'

'Ah yes, of course,' replied Bernard with a smile. 'How exciting for you. It's a time of great disarray in the Society of Magicians. The split in our community has been felt by magicians right around the world. We could do with some firm leadership. Something tells me you'll be just the man. Now, a cup of tea I think, Orson?'

'I'm all right,' said Orson, pinching another chocolate biscuit. 'I better head back up to my room.'

Magnus shook Orson's hand again. 'Nice to meet you, Orson. I'll see you later. I'm presiding over your ceremony.'

'Oh, brilliant!' said Orson. 'I can't wait. See you then.'

The father and son left together without another word.

Orson went back to his room for a shower before meeting Agatha in the lobby. 'Where to first?' he asked her, buttoning up his coat.

Brochure in her hand, Agatha showed Orson a picture of an imposing castle with massive stone walls. 'Edinburgh Castle,' she replied. Her eyes scanned the writing below the photograph. 'It's built on top of an extinct volcano called Castle Rock. What do you reckon?'

'Sounds good to me,' said Orson.

Twenty minutes later, after walking along a street known as the Royal Mile, in the heart of Edinburgh's Old Town, they were on the castle grounds. It was a cold and crisp day with a glaring sun, and Orson shielded his eyes as he made his way towards the castle entrance.

On his way into the castle, Orson saw a family of four gathered around an iron fountain. He could hear the family talking and, just by eavesdropping, he discovered that the fountain was called 'The Witches' Well' and was erected in 1894.

When the family departed a moment later, Orson moved closer to the fountain and began to read a bronze plaque positioned above it. The words made him shiver.

The ground on which he now stood was near the site that once saw hundreds of people, mostly women, burnt at the stake, between the fifteenth and eighteenth centuries. Erected in 1912, the plaque honoured their memory.

This grim story was familiar to Orson. He had already read about it in the book on secret societies. However, it was one thing reading about it, and another matter entirely actually being at the spot. Standing on an actual site where these atrocities had happened made the whole horrible story more real.

During the past centuries, anyone could be accused of black magic, witchcraft or sorcery and would be routinely sentenced to death. Orson felt sick.

Putting his hands together, he said a prayer, and felt thankful that he'd been granted an opportunity to pay his respects to the memory of these poor people. He blessed himself and left in a quiet reverence.

Inside, the historic castle was busy with many people still on their Christmas holidays and making the most of their free time.

Agatha quickly booked a tour and soon she and Orson were following their guide – a young lady called Rebecca, who lived in Edinburgh – around the magnificent castle.

For the next hour, they were led by Rebecca through the different parts of the castle, including the Royal Palace, the Great Hall – where there were many suits of armour – and St Margaret's Chapel, which Orson discovered was built in 1130 and was the oldest building in Edinburgh.

They walked underneath the portcullis gate, and the spikes reminded Orson of a dangerous machine that he'd seen in the Centre of Excellence back home.

To round off the tour, Orson and Agatha followed their group up the seventy steps of Lang Stairs and climbed to the summit of Castle Rock, overlooking the sweeping views of the city and beyond!

Orson stood with his hands resting on the wall, gazing out at the stunning sights of Scotland's capital city. The wind whistled in his ears, but overall the conditions of the day were favourable. Indeed, with such clear visibility, he swore he could see the highlands in the distance.

When they had soaked up the panoramic views for long enough, Orson walked back down the Lang Stairs alongside Agatha.

As they left the castle, Rebecca paused by the main gate and pointed to two statues positioned on either side of the entrance.

'Sir William Wallace and Robert the Bruce,' she explained to the group. 'These statues were added to the castle in 1929. Both men were leaders during the First War of Scottish Independence, which began in 1296.'

Orson found it fascinating to think about the year 1296. To even begin to imagine what life must've been like back then was mind boggling.

Anyway, he learnt that Robert the Bruce was the King of Scotland from 1306 until his death in 1329, and that William Wallace led an uprising against King Edward I of England. When William Wallace won the Battle of Stirling Bridge in 1297, he was knighted.

Orson turned to Agatha. 'Sounds like it would make a good movie one day!' he told her.

When the guided tour was over, Orson thanked Rebecca, before he and Agatha walked back into the city. It was now late in the afternoon and Orson's thoughts had already started to turn to his inauguration ceremony.

However, they squeezed lots more into the short time that they were in the city. Just by chance, they came upon a free museum and, once inside, they saw many works of decorative art and discovered more about Scotland's rich history.

They looked around shops and enjoyed a sumptuous three-course meal for a bargain price in an up-market restaurant that was situated down a narrow alleyway. Finally, after spending some time looking around the city's medieval architecture, they ended their tour of Edinburgh by strolling along the cobbled streets.

Eventually, without even realising it, they were gradually walking back in the direction of their hotel.

Orson had had one eye on his wristwatch ever since he'd left the castle and he'd grown more nervous about the ceremony as the day had gone on. Now that it was almost six o'clock in the evening it was all he could think of.

'You're very nervous, aren't you, Orson?' said Agatha, looking at him.

'You can tell?' answered Orson with a grimace.

Agatha smiled. 'William Wallace wouldn't get nervous.'

Orson laughed. 'No, he probably wouldn't.'

'You don't have to perform any magic,' Agatha told him. 'You just have to smile and sign the contract. Job done! I'm your assistant, aren't I?'

'You are,' said Orson.

'Then I'm telling you,' cried Agatha. 'Snap out of it. Just enjoy the night. You're about to become the Grand Master!'

Orson smiled. Agatha was spot on. He really didn't have to be nervous, and far greater challenges lay ahead. The closer he got to his hotel, the more confident he became. It was time for his alter ego to take over.

'I'm heading down early,' Agatha told him. 'Just to make sure that everything is running smoothly and that I get my hands on a copy of the schedule. I'll brief you later.'

Orson fought back a smile.

'What?' said Agatha, narrowing her eyes.

Orson laughed out loud. 'Brief me? You've really got the lingo down now.'

'Go get changed,' said Agatha with a smile.

A short time later, Orson went into his room and got changed into his suit for the evening. He laid the mystery box on his bed and stood before a mirror to make final adjustments to his glistening white shirt.

He opened the top button of his shirt, then closed it, before deciding to return it to its original state. After close inspection, he felt happy with that decision. He pulled on his jacket and straightened it.

It was showtime.

CHAPTER NINETEEN

The Clown

Orson entered the conference room around half past seven, but Agatha, in keeping with her promise, was already there mingling with people.

Orson was delighted to see her. To have a friend by his side when there were so many unfamiliar faces about was comforting, especially since his father couldn't be here.

When Agatha spotted Orson, she halted her conversation with Magnus and came rushing over to him.

'I'll take that,' she said, nodding at the mystery box clutched in Orson's hands.

Showing his complete faith in Agatha, Orson handed her the mystery box, which he did without so much as a second thought. Off she went with it up the stairs to the stage, leaving Orson to look around.

The hotel's conference room was packed, with barely a free seat available now. Standing up straight and tall, Orson walked further inside and all eyes turned to him.

It might as well have been a 'sales meeting', as all the people seated and those few still standing around talking were dressed casually in flared jeans, slim-fitting shirts, tank tops or turtle necks. There wasn't a top hat or a black cutaway coat between them. Nobody resembled a magician.

Agatha was back in a flash, smiling at him. 'Right,' she said. 'Let me sum this up.'

'Okay,' said Orson, looking up at the stage.

Agatha nodded. 'You're going to be introduced at eight o'clock. Then—'

'That doesn't give us much time,' said Orson, looking at his wristwatch. 'What else?'

Agatha rolled her eyes. 'I was just about to tell you before you interrupted me.'

'Sorry,' said Orson, holding his hand up.

'Once you go up on stage,' said Agatha fastidiously, 'Magnus will say how wonderful you are, and then you sign the contract. After that, Magnus puts the pin on your jacket, you smile and bow, and then it's over! Simple.'

Orson nodded at Agatha. It did sound simple when she phrased it like that.

'Okay,' said Orson. 'But shouldn't we stay for the refreshments afterwards?'

Agatha looked annoyed with herself. 'Sorry, my fault. After you smile and bow, you go get some refreshments, talk to a few people and then it's over!'

On the stroke of eight o'clock, Magnus came walking over to Orson and smiled. 'Let's get you up on stage. There's a contract waiting to be signed.'

'Good luck,' said Agatha.

'Thanks,' replied Orson. Then he followed Magnus up the steps and onto the stage. He sat down at a table upon Magnus' request, lifted the contract and tried to read all the small print as quickly as he could.

As Orson did this, Magnus began to speak. 'Our new Grand Master,' he declared, beginning to applaud.

The people in the audience stood and applauded with him.

When the applause had diminished, Orson lifted the pen and moved it towards the line marked, GRAND MASTER'S SIGNATURE:

_____

'Extra points if you can make the pen disappear,' said Magnus.

Orson looked over his shoulder.

'Joke,' said Magnus, laughing.

Orson smiled. There was far too much small print at the bottom of the contract for him to get through. Moreover, the font size was practically unreadable. He could hardly start squinting at it now. Not with everyone waiting expectantly for him to sign his name. So he didn't read it and scribbled his name on the allotted line.

The crowd began to applaud.

Orson stood up.

From the mystery box, Magnus removed the gold pin and fastened it onto Orson's jacket. Another rapturous applause reverberated around the conference suite.

Magnus then presented Orson with a black cane that had a silver skull at its top.

Orson held the cane in his two hands. It was identical to every other cane he'd seen. It was all very official now. He was looking around for somewhere to put the cane, when Agatha was suddenly by his side and taking it from him. He whispered his thanks to her.

Magnus was handed a microphone by a blonde-haired woman.

'Congratulations, Orson,' said Magnus, speaking into the microphone. 'It's been a turbulent last couple of years in the magic community. We've never been more divided. But, thanks to your appointment, I think we'll leave Edinburgh tonight with a lot more hope.'

Orson nodded and smiled.

Magnus looked out at the audience. 'Have a lovely evening, everybody. Please help yourselves to the refreshments and, God willing, we'll see you all on Christmas Eve! Have a great year. Drive safe. Thanks very much.'

Applause turned to cheers as Orson smiled and began to wave to the crowd. The whole thing was painless. Short and sweet, just as Agatha had promised it would be. He walked down the steps to many pats on the back, and he was made to feel very welcome as he went around the various tables with his plate for sandwiches, biscuits, buns and a glass of milk.

One of the first people he spoke to was a man named Albert Matthews, a friend of his father's.

'And how is your father?' asked Albert, offering his hand.

Orson shook Albert's hand. 'Much better, thankfully,' he told him. 'Recovering well. He wanted to be here, but it was just a little too soon for him.'

'No point rushing it,' agreed Albert. 'Well, tell him I was asking after him.'

Orson said that he would and was about to take a bite of a salad sandwich, when he heard a commotion a few places back in the queue.

A giant of a man was sparring with a much smaller guy. They were mimicking a boxing fight, but such was their size difference it looked a strange mismatch.

'In one corner,' bellowed the large man, 'we have the master of mind control, Daxton the Destroyer, and in the other, we have the child prodigy

Orson the Great! The fate of the magic community is on the line. It should be epic. Who will be crowned the champion?'

The small man, presumably doubling for Orson, suddenly took a simulated blow to the nose, which resulted in fake blood squirting to the floor.

Orson did find all this mildly amusing and stood looking at the strange duo's antics. He got the impression that they were a Laurel and Hardy tribute act, perhaps with a little magic mixed in with the comedy.

A different man, whose plate was piled high with cakes and biscuits, turned to Orson with a smile. 'They're a couple of circus magicians,' he said. 'A double act. The small guy deputises as the clown.'

This so-called clown wiped the fake blood from around his nose with a handkerchief and started laughing and pointing at Orson.

The big man introduced himself as Harry and shook Orson's hand. 'So, a Christmas Eve showdown! How dramatic. Just a head's up. This Daxton fellow is a psychopath. He will bring you down to the lowest level if he thinks it'll help him to win that.' He pointed to the pin on Orson's jacket.

The deputy clown said nothing, but nodded his head in agreement.

Harry laid a hand upon Orson's shoulder. 'Daxton only ever thinks about himself. If he wins, we'll never be able to remove him again. He's too brilliant a magician. He'll be Grand Master of the Society of Magicians for good. And that, Orson, my dear young man, would spell disaster for us all.'

Orson placed his salad sandwich down on a plate. 'Why?'

Magnus arrived and stood between Orson and Harry. 'Everything all right?'

'Harry was just telling me about Daxton,' said Orson, a look of concern on his face.

Magnus stared at Orson. 'I feel the loss of one of our own, but Harry is right. Daxton will stop at nothing to become the Grand Master. He feels it's his destiny. He's determined to seize control over the Society of Magicians, and anybody who stands in his way is in danger.'

'What could he do?' asked Orson innocently.

The clown produced from his pocket a pistol, pointed it at Orson and pulled the trigger. Out flew a red flag with the word 'BANG' written on it in black ink.

'It wouldn't come to that, would it?' asked Orson in a high-pitched voice.

Magnus said he wasn't so sure. 'Since the split in our society, journeymen magicians have tended to go missing. We can't prove it, of course, but we suspect Daxton is involved in their disappearance. All of those who have vanished were his fiercest critics.'

Orson felt the world closing in around him. This was a different level of threat altogether. It was one thing going up against a highly skilled magician, but it was another matter entirely taking on one who was doubling as a serial killer. Perhaps he should've read the small print of the contract, after all!

Harry was frowning. 'If you're not on his side, then you're a target. Any one of us here tonight could be next.'

'Just lay low until Christmas Eve,' said Magnus. 'Work hard on your routines, pit yourself against him next Christmas and give it your best shot! That's all you can do.'

Orson shook his head. 'Magnus, Christmas is eleven months away. Can you promise me I'll be safe until then?'

Magnus shook his head. 'Being honest, no I can't,' he replied mournfully. 'None of us are safe. "The Destroyer" has lost his mind!'

'So,' said Orson, 'what do I do if I see Daxton before now and Christmas Eve?'

'And he *will* try to find you!' said Harry, evading the answer. 'Nothing surer. There will be an attempt to steal the pin from you. He would rather do that, than risk his reputation by facing and potentially losing to you on stage in front of an audience of his peers!'

Orson tutted. 'So, what do I do?'

The clown, who Orson guessed never said a word as part of the double act, suddenly broke his vow of silence to offer up a piece of sage advice. 'If "The Destroyer" shows up, you run, boy. You run!'

CHAPTER TWENTY

Christmas, 1972

Orson fought with every fibre of his being and then some. Throwing his leg back, he managed to kick Daxton on the shin. To look a little taller for tonight's show, he'd chosen his shoes with the slightly larger heels and, boy, was he thankful he made that decision now.

Daxton rocked back. Just enough for Orson to free himself and gather Daxton's cane that had fallen on the floor. He lifted it and wacked Daxton across the head with the silver skull.

As he did this, he realised that it wasn't Daxton at all. The man who was attacking him was a red-haired henchman who obviously worked for 'The Destroyer'.

Orson sprinted towards the door and hurried out into the corridor. Not a moment later, the red-haired man jogged a little unsteadily after him.

Glancing over his shoulder, Orson saw Daxton's right-hand man stumbling along the corridor and bumping against the walls.

Orson knew that he'd obviously struck the man a powerful blow with the cane. Good! Knowing it would be too long a wait for the elevator, he shouldered open an emergency exit door and ran down the stairs.

Jumping the last few steps, he grabbed hold of the banister and descended the next set of stairs, thinking about Agatha as he went. He had to warn her. She could be next. What room was she staying in? It was on the second floor, but what was the room number?! Had she even told him? Think!

Orson had read many books on memory techniques. It was a useful tool in the magician's armoury. The techniques he learnt could be adapted and used to enhance many different routines in his show.

Anything from remembering the sequence of an entire deck of cards, to memorising long lists of random items compiled by a spectator were just some of the ways in which he used these methods to enhance his show.

So, he was adamant. Agatha hadn't told him her room number or else he would've remembered it. So where was he going? As far away from his own room as he could possibly get seemed like a pretty good idea.

Orson sprinted down the next corridor, just as the elevator doors on that floor opened. It had to be Daxton's gang of thugs, so he hid behind the wall. As expected, he saw several men dressed in black suits with canes clasped in their hands rushing out.

To Orson's surprise, they all went to their left, leaving the corridor and the elevator free. A brief opportunity had presented itself. He ran to the elevator, rushed inside and pressed the ground floor on the selection of buttons.

After what seemed like an eternity, the doors eventually closed with a beep and down he travelled. He straightened his jacket and tried to catch his breath.

When he reached the ground floor, the elevator beeped again, the doors parted and he ran straight over to the main reception.

Ms Ford placed her pen down and looked up. 'Mr Whitlock,' she cried. 'Is everything all right?'

Orson's face was flushed. 'No, everything's not all right!' he panted. 'I'm being attacked!'

Ms Ford's eyes widened. 'I beg your pardon? Did you just say you were—'

'Attacked!' shrieked Orson. 'There are people after me! They broke into my room.'

'Who's in your room?' said Ms Ford, remaining calm.

'A man dressed in a black suit,' cried Orson in an agitated state. 'But there are even more of these thugs running around. They probably have the hotel surrounded! They're carrying black canes, and the man in control of them is a complete psychopath. Call the police!'

Ms Ford reached for the phone beside her, but hesitated.

'Please, Ms Ford!' begged Orson.

Ms Ford lifted the phone and dialled a number. 'I tell you what. I'll call security. They'll have a look around!'

'Call the police as well!' cried Orson urgently. 'Your hotel is under attack!'

As Ms Ford calmly explained the situation to a security person on the phone, Orson took a look around the deserted lobby. It was late. This was turning into an awful night. He was facing the biggest day of his life tomorrow and this was his preparation – a night of disrupted sleep and constant worry.

He was beginning to think that 'Daxton the Destroyer' wasn't here at all. Perhaps Daxton's henchmen were sent into the hotel to deprive him of sleep, so that he'd arrive to the contest tomorrow completely exhausted. If that was indeed the plan that had been hatched by Daxton, then it was working perfectly.

Ms Ford hung up the phone. 'Security are sending someone over.' She smiled at Orson and then returned to her work, as if the emergency was all but over in her eyes. The little Christmas song that she began humming to herself seemed to confirm this.

A gruff-looking, middle-aged man strolled into the lobby, looking half-asleep and a little annoyed to have been called into action. He had a large moustache, bushy eyebrows and a terrible complexion.

Orson felt woefully underwhelmed by this security man. He looked at the revolving doors that led outside. Even at this late hour, would he be better served to try his luck with another hotel?

'Are you the magician?' asked the security man.

If Orson hadn't been recognised, he most likely would've bolted out the front door, but now he felt obliged to cooperate. 'Yeah,' he said angrily. 'Yeah, I am.'

'It could be a party,' said the security man, walking towards the elevator. 'They can make far too much noise sometimes when they come in from a late night out.'

Orson shook his head and heaved a deep sigh. 'It's not a party! You are listening to me, aren't you? I've explained this already. A man just broke into my room and tried to kidnap me.'

The security man gave a quick nod. 'You need to relax. Just listen to my voice and, as you do, you'll find yourself becoming more and more relaxed.'

Orson stepped into the cabin of the elevator, the security man following, and pushed the number 'five' on the floor selection buttons. The lights were flickering. Dark one moment, bright the next.

The elevator stopped on the third floor and the doors slid open.

Nobody.

Whoever had requested the elevator was no longer there, and if they were then they'd somehow managed to invent invisibility.

If the latter was indeed the case, then Orson wanted to meet this person and ask him or her some important questions. A superpower like invisibility would add so much to his routine.

These silly thoughts were floating around in Orson's mind, when a more pertinent one surfaced. 'What are you going to do if they're still in my room?' he said to the security man.

The security man said nothing.

'You'll have to call for backup!' Orson told him firmly. 'You've got no idea the type of man you're dealing with! Are you listening to me? What's your name?'

There was no reply.

Orson sighed in exasperation. 'I said—'

Just then, something landed on the floor of the elevator next to him and he recoiled in horror. Looking closer, he saw the man's face on the floor! His very face! The pale skin, the moustache and the bushy eyebrows were all there! And a black wig next to that! What was going on?

A terrible sense of dread came over Orson as he turned around. It was dark as he did so, but when the light flicked on a moment later, he saw the face of his rival looking down at him.

Daxton laid a hand upon Orson's shoulder. 'And sleep.'

Orson fought it, but his eyes flickered.

'Sleep,' said Daxton again.

This time, Orson's eyes closed and his chin fell onto his chest.

CHAPTER TWENTY-ONE

An Insurance Policy

In the deep recesses of his mind, Orson heard a clap and awoke slowly.

'And you're back in the room,' said Daxton softly.

Orson was back in his hotel room, but he was also chained to a post by handcuffs.

Daxton sat pensively on a chair about five yards away. Like a spy in an espionage movie, he peeled the remnants of the rubber mask off his neck. His trademark cane with a skull at its top was propped against the chair. He seized the cane and pointed it at Orson.

'It's been a while since you and I last spoke,' he said calmly.

Orson shook his head, annoyed at himself. He hadn't seen Daxton in almost a year; but, even allowing for that fact, he'd been complacent.

Over the months since his inauguration in Edinburgh, he'd gradually got used to his newfound fame and he'd let his guard down. Well, it had come back to haunt him. Daxton had timed his ambush to perfection.

'You have something that belongs to me,' said Daxton, standing up.

Orson looked down at the shiny gold pin on his jacket. He knew that Daxton could've taken it by now, but 'The Destroyer' had obviously waited to gloat.

Orson smiled. 'Keep it safe for me. This time tomorrow night, the pin will be back on my jacket!'

With a smile, Daxton removed the pin from Orson's jacket and attached it to his own. 'I like your confidence. An essential trait for any magician.'

'I will beat you!' predicted Orson, glaring at Daxton.

Daxton shrugged. 'You should thank me,' he declared. 'I'm doing you a favour.'

'How are you doing me a favour?' cried Orson, reddening with rage.

Daxton shrugged. 'I'm now the Grand Master. Ask any competitor. You're more motivated to reclaim a prize than retain it!' He turned to leave. 'This will only spur you on tomorrow.'

'That's it?' cried Orson furiously. 'That's what all this was about? Becoming the Grand Master before tomorrow?'

Daxton nodded and pulled on a pair of black gloves. 'Of course. Why? Did you think this was personal? It's not. I'm a practical man. The pin is my insurance policy.'

The red-haired man, whom Orson had grappled with earlier, now walked tentatively into the room with a pronounced limp. A dirty look was cast Orson's way before he spoke.

'We should go, Grand Master,' he said reverently.

Daxton smiled. 'Of course. Big day coming up! It should be an amazing contest. Don't you agree, Orson?' He pulled on his black overcoat and, with the aid of his cane, he began to walk towards the door. 'I can't wait.'

Orson strained to get out of the handcuffs, but it was no use. 'What?!' he shouted in a wild rage. 'You're just going to leave me here? How will I get out? Daxton!'

Daxton turned around. From the deep pocket of his overcoat, he removed a gold key and flung it on the carpet.

Orson knew the key was much too far away for him to reach it.

'You'll be able to leave this room,' said Daxton, 'whenever you decide that you want to be free.'

Daxton J. Auger, professionally known as 'Daxton the Destroyer', smiled smugly. He was now the Grand Master of the Society of Magicians, a title he had coveted his entire life.

'One day you'll thank me for all of this,' he said, fixing the collar of his coat as he glanced back at Orson. 'I promise.'

And then, without looking back, the new Grand Master left the room.

CHAPTER TWENTY-TWO

A Time To Reflect

Orson was lying down on the floor with his legs extended out before him. Stretching his body as far as he could, he strained to reach the key with his right foot, but it remained, cruelly, just out of his reach. Of course it did. Daxton knew what he was doing.

The reality of the whole situation hit Orson like a sledgehammer. Daxton had played him like a fool. And he was one! A cocky, arrogant fool who had believed his own hype.

Magnus had told him to keep a low profile. Instead, he'd used the last few months to make a name for himself. January, February and March were fine. He had worked hard in the Centre of Excellence, developing strategies and innovative ways to perform his routines.

It was a balancing act combining his magic with his schoolwork, but somehow he'd managed it. He was already starting to make a name for himself amongst his circle of friends when he took his magic onto the street over the Easter holidays.

He performed a variety of routines to unwitting members of the public in some of London's busiest streets. Taking his magic into the public domain had an immediate effect.

A fortuitous encounter with a reporter on Oxford Street had paved the way for Orson's success. The mind control trick he'd played on an unsuspecting group of American tourists made the main evening news. From that point on, it was difficult to turn the offers and the money down.

Agatha had also liaised with contacts within the Society of Magicians to open a few doors. She had felt that Orson shouldn't waste the exciting marketing opportunities that a slot on the news had presented him with.

Besides, in order to bring his vision to the stage, he needed the money. As his fame grew, so too did the scale of his show. He had travel and production costs to cover. After all, an orchestra and a special effects unit didn't come cheap.

Agatha devised a marketing strategy and Orson stuck to it. He appeared on children's television, cut ribbons at service station openings, became the face of a breakfast cereal and was a brand ambassador for a car company, even though he was too young to drive.

If Orson was being honest with himself, he had enjoyed the limelight and was more than happy to capitalise on his newfound celebrity status.

During all this time, he had put Daxton and the Christmas Eve showdown to the back of his mind. It had caught up with him now!

He wished he could go back and do things differently, but he couldn't. All his efforts this year, all the wrong decisions he'd made, had led to this moment – being handcuffed to a post in his hotel suite.

Of course, Agatha would come looking for him eventually, but by then he'd have to get a later taxi. Then it would be a mad hurry to the venue, without any preparation, before taking to the stage in a fluster. He had to escape!

He kicked off one of his shoes and tried to use it as a device to reach the key. He tried over and over again. He got closer each time, but he wasn't quite able to reach it.

Exhausted, he turned his attention to the handcuffs. In the absence of a key, he needed a paperclip or a sharp instrument of some description. He knew how it worked – if he had a paperclip, he could pull a screw from the locking mechanism and the handcuffs would click open.

Ah, he had had enough! He gave up and sat down to stretch out his legs, which he did with a sigh. What a sorry sight. 'Orson the Great' lying on the carpet of his hotel room handcuffed to a post. If the judges of the contest could see him now, they'd hand Daxton the title of Grand Master before either of them had stepped foot on stage.

With tears forming in his eyes, Orson thought about his family. He wanted to make them all proud. He knew his grandparents were coming to watch his performance.

His grandfather had even bought a new suit for the event and his grandmother had booked an appointment to get her hair done. His father had recovered from a serious operation and would obviously be there, too.

Resting his head back against the post, Orson thought about his mum. If he somehow managed to free himself, then he was going to tell her everything. He was going to show her the Centre of Excellence and he would make sure she came to watch him tomorrow.

Tears began to stream down his face. She was the greatest mum in the world. How could he perform in a vital contest without his mum being there? He couldn't!

Winning back the leadership of the Society of Magicians would feel worthless, anyway, without his mum there to see it. If he was going to win his title back, he wanted his mum there!

The image of Uncle Tom flashed in his mind's eye and he smiled to himself. What a lovely man his uncle was. If, by some miracle, he managed to get himself out of this dire situation, and if God Almighty was asking him the question, then yes, he would invite Uncle Tom, too.

With his vision blurred by tears, Orson gazed at the key on the carpet. Throwing his head back against the post, he sighed. Then he hit the post with his head once more, listening. He narrowed his eyes.

There was a very hollow sound to the post. Moreover, it was a lot softer than what you'd expect a wooden post to feel like. Was it even made of wood?

The more he thought about it, the less sure he was that this post had even been in his room earlier. He got to his feet and ran the handcuffs upwards. The post travelled all the way up to the ceiling, but it looked more like a prop of some description.

He had a sinking feeling as he ran the handcuffs further up and found a little groove through which he was able to slip the handcuffs free. What a fool Daxton was making of him. He'd been so preoccupied with the handcuffs and, perhaps even more so, with the key on the floor that he hadn't even thought of checking the actual post.

It was classic misdirection and he'd fallen for it. Of course he had. Daxton was beating him, all ends up. To stand any chance tomorrow, he needed to start thinking more clearly.

Wriggling his fingers behind his back, Orson knelt down and lifted the gold key. It was highly unlikely that Daxton had left the correct key. Why would he?

To Orson's shock, placing the key in the lock and expecting nothing to happen, he discovered that it did indeed fit and the handcuffs opened with a click.

Rubbing his wrists, he sat down upon the bed, giving himself a moment to take stock of everything.

That was the last time Daxton would have fun at his expense. It was time to take back control. Orson switched on a light by his bed and went into the living room quarters through the connecting door.

At that moment, Big Ben chimed outside and, by the lights of the two Christmas trees in the room, Orson saw on the clock on the wall that it was three in the morning.

Exhausted, he went back into his bedroom and, without changing into his pyjamas, he threw himself down on the mattress. It was the early hours of Christmas Eve. His day of destiny had arrived. He got goosebumps just thinking about it.

As he fell asleep, his last thoughts were of Daxton and the mouth-watering showdown that awaited him later that day.

CHAPTER TWENTY-THREE

The Sleepwalker

And his first thoughts when he awoke, five hours later, were of Daxton and the mouth-watering showdown that awaited later that day. Two magicians at the top of their profession, vying for the ultimate prize in magic. It was difficult not to be excited now.

After a shower, Orson got dressed into a pair of jeans, a white shirt and a red jacket before making his way downstairs into the restaurant for breakfast. He found himself a table by the window and hung his jacket on the back of the chair.

As he poured himself a glass of orange juice, he saw Agatha coming towards him.

'Oh, hey,' she said, sitting down opposite him.

'Morning,' replied Orson with a tired smile. 'Merry Christmas.'

Agatha laughed. 'Merry Christmas to you, too. Gosh, it's hard to believe it's Christmas Eve!' She looked strangely at him. 'You look tired. Did you not sleep well?'

Orson shook his head. 'No, not really. You?'

'Like a baby!' replied Agatha, helping herself to a glass of cranberry juice.

Orson saw Ms Ford at the opposite side of the restaurant. She was doing her rounds of the tables. Orson locked eyes with her and she came walking over with a huge grin on her face.

'How are you feeling this morning, Mr Whitlock?' she asked cheerily.

'Fine,' said Orson. 'Just fine. Sorry about last night. I'd a bad dream and I was sleepwalking. Happens sometimes after a show.'

Agatha choked on her cranberry juice. 'You were sleepwalking last night?'

Orson nodded. 'I was a little confused, but—'

'He thought the hotel was under siege!' cried Ms Ford, digging Agatha in the ribs with her elbow. 'He wanted me to call the police.'

'And did you?' asked Agatha, wiping cranberry juice from her chin with a napkin.

'No, I did not,' said Ms Ford, hooting with laughter. 'I shouldn't laugh, but I knew he was dreaming. I sent Stephen up with him to have a look in his room.'

'Oh, okay,' said Agatha. 'Is Stephen the security man?'

Ms Ford motioned her hand in the direction of the security man named Stephen, who was standing in the corner of the restaurant with his arms folded. 'The strange thing is, though,' she added, 'Stephen has absolutely no recollection of meeting Mr Whitlock last night.'

'Well, he wouldn't,' said Orson, turning around in his chair to take a good look at Stephen. He noted the pale skin, black hair, and the busy moustache. He knew, there and then, that Daxton could add master of disguise to his many talents. Daxton's disguise last night was uncanny.

Ms Ford looked at Orson, then over at Stephen. 'Oh, really? Why not?'

'I hypnotised him,' replied Orson with a wink and a smile.

Ms Ford waved a hand at Orson and broke into a fit of hysterical laughter that caused everyone in the restaurant to turn around and look over at her.

'Stop!' she gasped. She then turned to Agatha. 'Such a charmer. I can see why your boyfriend is so famous.'

Agatha rolled her eyes. 'He's not my—'

It was too late. Ms Ford had gone over to table thirty-nine to wish a family she knew a Merry Christmas.

'What really happened last night?' asked Agatha, talking over another round of Ms Ford's shrill laughter.

Orson shook his head. 'Ah, it doesn't matter. Can I ask you a question?'

Agatha nodded as she poured milk into her cereal. 'Go on.'

'Did you tell me what room number you were staying in last night?' asked Orson.

Agatha shook her head, a puzzled look upon her face. 'Er, I don't think so. Why?'

'Doesn't matter,' said Orson.

Agatha was crunching on her cereal. 'What *does* matter, though, is "Orson the Great" versus "Daxton the Destroyer". You're not nervous, are you?'

Orson shook his head and asked Agatha to pass over the jug of milk. 'Too tired right now to be nervous,' he said, taking hold of the jug.

'Well, I am!' said Agatha, grimacing.

Orson smiled at her as he poured milk over his cereal. 'We've done a show like this loads of times,' he told her. 'In front of larger audiences and in bigger venues.'

Agatha perked up. 'Fair point. Right, listen up. The itinerary.' She placed a file on the table and removed a sheet of paper from it. Running her finger down the page, she showed Orson the list of tricks, illusions and mentalism acts that he had planned to conjure up for the evening's performance.

'We agreed this list weeks ago,' said Orson, his eyes scanning the familiar sequence of tricks.

'We did,' said Agatha timidly. 'I'm just checking that you don't want to make any last-minute additions or changes. You're happy with it?'

Orson nodded. 'Very.'

'Good,' said Agatha. 'Next on the agenda.' From the file, she removed another sheet of paper entitled 'TOP SECRET'. It contained details about the evening's contest compiled by the organisers. 'This is your copy.' She lowered her glasses onto the bridge of her nose and looked at Orson pointedly. 'Are you getting all this?'

With a beaming smile, Orson replied, 'Yes. I'm listening.'

'Good,' said Agatha. 'So, the taxi is at half past eleven. Then home for a couple of hours to relax. You need to be at the hotel no later than five o'clock to get set up. I'll be there at four forty-five, so ideally we should meet at that time.'

Orson nodded. When the waitress came over, he ordered a full English breakfast, whereas Agatha chose scrambled egg and toast with mushrooms and grilled tomatoes. When she had finished her breakfast, Agatha went back upstairs to her room to finish packing.

Orson wiped his mouth with a napkin and sat quietly. He turned to his right and locked eyes with a boy at a nearby table who was roughly a year or two younger than him. The boy might very well have recognised him from the show last night. This was starting to happen quite a bit now. Sometimes, he could hardly believe how much his life had changed.

Whatever happened tonight, he would feel proud of the progress he'd made in such a short space of time. Win or lose, magic was going to be his future.

From his pocket, Orson produced a light-brown envelope and took from it the king of hearts. In the king's hand was the six of spades. It was the card that had kickstarted this incredible adventure for him.

With a smile, he resealed the card inside the envelope and slipped it into the back pocket of his trousers. He got up and, upon request from the boy's mother, he scribbled his signature on the front cover of last night's programme.

Orson eyed his image on the cover. The photograph had been taken a few months ago during his tour of Ireland, in a packed Galway theatre. He had his arms outstretched, accepting the round of applause from the audience.

'Orson the Great' was written across the top of the programme in large, capital letters. After wishing the mother and her son a Merry Christmas, Orson left the restaurant and went back upstairs to his room.

There were no nerves. Just a determined focus.

He was going to win this evening.

He was sure of it!

CHAPTER
TWENTY-FOUR

Three Generations of Whitlocks

To allow for the heavy Christmas Eve traffic, the taxi left a little earlier than expected. When it arrived at Paddington station, his mum, as dependable as always, was there waiting for him.

A very nervous-looking Agatha was picked up by her dad. However, before she and Orson had departed, they had arranged to meet up again at four forty-five at the venue.

'How was the tour?' asked Orson's mum, when he had got into the car and they were on their way home.

Orson sighed. 'It was great, but I'm happy to be heading home. Long time away. I missed you, Mum.'

'Well, I missed you too, Orson,' replied his mum. 'You're performing again this evening, aren't you?'

Orson looked over at his mum in surprise. What exactly had his mum been told about this evening's event?

'I am,' he said succinctly. 'Are you coming to watch me?'

'I wouldn't miss it for the world!' replied his mum, exiting a roundabout.

Orson knew, then and there, that his mum *didn't* know the full story about the evening's event, at all.

He wanted to tell his mum everything – that he had spent the last two years of his life working towards this event and that the majority of the members of the Society of Magicians were counting on him to defeat Daxton.

'Great,' he said finally when he realised his mum wasn't going to say anything further on the matter.

When they got home, Orson got a quick bite to eat and, afterwards, he went into his dad's workshop. He removed the English dictionary, then shoved it back into the space where he'd taken it from.

The bookshelf clicked open and he walked inside. After climbing the spiral staircase, he went across the balcony, rested his hands on the balustrade and looked down at the Centre of Excellence.

Most of the equipment had already been removed to that evening's venue. He climbed down the ladder for a closer look and was walking idly about when he heard footsteps.

'Say it and mean it,' said his father, stepping from the shadows and standing next to his son.

Orson turned to face his dad. 'I believe in magic.'

'I had a feeling you'd come here,' said his dad. 'You nervous?'

Orson shook his head. 'Dad, I'm not nervous. I'm ready.'

His father nodded. 'You are.'

'Mum knows about tonight, Dad.'

'She does,' said Orson's dad, nodding. 'But nothing has been left to chance. The Society of Magicians has marketed this evening's contest as a magic convention. It's a free event, open to the public and with you and Daxton preforming for "fun". When you and Daxton have finished your head-to-head performances, the judges in the crowd will vote for their winner.'

Orson raised his eyebrows. 'That simple, huh?'

'That simple,' said his dad.

'I want to tell Mum the truth,' said Orson. 'I don't want any more secrets. I think she should know about the Society of Magicians.'

Orson's dad nodded. 'Fair enough. After the contest, we'll tell her together.'

'Thanks, Dad,' said Orson. 'Is Tom coming to the contest?'

'I'm afraid not,' replied his dad. 'I invited him, obviously, but he's working late in the office. Something about a broken fax machine.'

Orson shrugged. 'Oh, right. These things can happen.' He looked up at the framed photograph of his father, grandfather and Daxton on the wall.

Daxton, beardless and fresh-faced, seemed to return the gaze.

'Don't let Daxton get in your head,' said his dad. 'You owe it to yourself not to let that happen.'

'I won't,' said Orson, his eyes moist.

'Daxton will try everything to beat you,' his dad continued. 'Expect anything. If he parades an elephant out on stage and makes it disappear, you shouldn't be surprised.'

Orson didn't need to be told.

His dad smiled. 'Whatever happens this evening, Orson, your mother and I will be very proud of you.'

Orson fell into his dad's arms in tears. He didn't even know why he was suddenly so upset. Enveloped in his father's embrace, the magnitude of the impending task suddenly dawned on him.

The evening's contest wasn't just about him; he was fighting for three generations of Whitlocks. He was picking up the mantle and, for the first time, he was starting to feel the pressure of it all.

Martin Whitlock wiped away the tears on Orson's cheeks. 'We'll see you after,' he said with a kind smile. 'No more tears. Just do your best.'

Orson knew he couldn't let his father down. This meant everything to his dad. To ensure his family's future, he had to win!

He just had to.

CHAPTER TWENTY-FIVE

Orson vs Daxton

'ORSON THE GREAT' VS 'DAXTON THE DESTROYER'

The three hundred-foot banner draped over the walls of the hotel said it all. Just below the words was an image of Orson and Daxton dressed in their finest suits and facing each other, like two boxers before a bout. The stage was set.

The nerves finally kicked in when Orson got out of his mum's car and saw people of all ages entering the venue.

'Nice photo of you,' said Grace Whitlock, popping her head out the window and looking up at the banner.

Orson raised his eyes and took another look at the banner. He usually hated looking at photos of himself, but, on this occasion, he had to agree with his mum. It *was* a good photo of him.

His mum was off to the shops to buy provisions for Christmas. She seemed more concerned about the lack of gravy in the house for dinner later that evening than she was about her son's upcoming contest.

Orson had to smile. There he was, caught up in his own troubles, and yet his mum was consumed by her own problems. And what made his concerns more important than hers? Nothing, he knew. Absolutely nothing!

Orson's shoes crunched on the snow-kissed ground as he made the short walk to the doors of the hotel and then into the lobby. It wasn't packed, but there were definite signs of what was to come in just over an hour's time.

There were people dressed alike in fine suits, and there were children garbed in capes and top hats, brandishing their magic wands around and pretending to cast spells on whoever dared to look their way.

Several carollers were also assembled there, singing away to their heart's content, with baskets by their feet half full of money for their chosen charity.

Orson found a shiny new ten pound note deep inside his trouser pocket, walked over to the carollers and threw his contribution into the basket before them.

Beside the carollers, Orson saw a large poster perched upon a stand with arrows directing people to different areas of the hotel. With his hands on his hips, he took a moment to peruse it.

A Christmas fair in aid of charity was around the next corner on the left. Mince pies, mulled wine and other festive treats were available to the public in a room to the right. The carollers remained in the lobby, while those wanting to attend the 'Magic convention' were pointed in the direction of the adjoining corridor.

As the carollers sang 'Have Yourself A Merry Little Christmas', Orson followed the direction of the arrow pointing him towards the 'Magic convention'.

When he pushed through the doors, he saw stalls of magic memorabilia and all kinds of artefacts assembled along the corridor preceding the venue. It was a shrine to a bygone era with props and gimmicks from the 'Golden Age' of magic.

Orson had read about this in a book once. He knew that this period spanned from the 1880s to the 1930s, when magicians were commercially very successful and achieved unprecedented levels of fame and success.

Even at a glance, Orson could tell that some of the items in the display were very impressive indeed, but he was much too focused now to care about any of it.

As he walked along the corridor, he saw Agatha hurrying over to him.

She was all in a panic, looking flushed and out of breath. 'The conductor has just told me,' she gasped, 'that we've lost twenty orchestra members.'

'Twenty?' cried Orson.

'Yes,' replied Agatha. 'There isn't a single cello player left. It's Christmas Eve and they had other plans.'

'We'll manage,' said Orson with a determined nod. 'Is there anything else?'

Agatha nodded. 'Ralph said he wants double pay, or else he won't stay around, either, to do the gig.'

Orson rolled his eyes. 'Typical Ralph.'

'I know,' said Agatha. 'But I think he's bluffing. The contract has been signed. We'll be able to sue him for breach of contract. He can't just leave.'

'Look, tell him that's fine,' said Orson. 'Keep him onside. Anything else I should know about?'

Agatha nodded. 'There are no special effects or lighting units allowed on stage. I've sent some of the stagehands home, but I paid them in full because it was very late notice.'

'That's only fair,' said Orson.

Agatha raised her finger and pointed to a door about halfway down the corridor. 'C'mon, your dressing room is through that door.'

As he followed Agatha along the corridor, Orson caught a glimpse, through a half-opened door, of the actual venue. There was a large stage with a massive screen behind it. Fairly typical for a magic show.

The auditorium itself had around two hundred and fifty seats laid out with additional space for people to stand at the back if they so wished. It was impressive, but nothing that Orson hadn't seen or performed in many times before.

The en suite dressing room was spacious and he said as much to Agatha as they walked inside and had a good look around. His dry-cleaned suit and some of his essential inventory awaited him in a locker. He sat down on a bench and took a deep breath.

Agatha fixed her glasses and removed a sheet of paper from the competition pack she was holding. She was about to read from it, when suddenly there came a knock upon the door.

Orson got to his feet. 'Come in.'

A small, austere-looking man, donned in a sparkling white suit, came in with a clipboard in his hands. He apologised for the intrusion before handing Orson a sheet of paper. 'Here's the schedule of events, Mr Whitlock. Be sure to have a good look at it.'

'Who are you?' asked Orson, looking at the man after he'd scanned the bullet points on the sheet of paper.

'I'm Peter.'

Agatha swiped the sheet of paper off Orson and compared it with her own document.

'You'll notice a slight change, Ms Anderson,' said Peter robustly. 'There will be a coin toss to see who performs first.' He looked Orson up and down. 'Casual wear is not permitted.'

Orson forced a smile. 'Yeah, I know. I was just about to get changed.'

'About to get changed, isn't changed, Mr Whitlock,' said Peter sharply. 'Strict dress code from this point onwards. You'll need to be in your formal wear for the coin toss at five fifteen. You'll be disqualified if you're not appropriately dressed by then.'

Peter took another dismissive look at Orson's blue jeans. Then he left without another word.

'He's a barrel of laughs,' said Agatha.

'Gosh, I'd better get changed,' said Orson, glancing up at the clock on the wall and seeing that it was almost five o'clock.

'Me too,' said Agatha. 'The same format as the Paris show, then?'

Orson nodded. Why would he change the routine now? He had a show that would beat nearly all other magicians on the circuit. He hated those two dreadful words right now – 'nearly all'. As in 'nearly all' magicians except Daxton? He knew he would soon find out the answer to that question.

'Right, I'm off to get changed,' said Agatha, hurrying towards the door.

'Where are my shoes with—' said Orson, but Agatha had already left.

He rummaged in a locker and found the size seven shoes with the long heels. Looking taller tonight beside a man who was well over six feet in height was essential. After locking his dressing room door, he transformed into 'Orson the Great' in no time.

Black suit, freshly ironed white shirt with single cuffs, tailored navy-blue waistcoat, red bow tie – he really was dressed to kill. A little gel on the hair and he was all set.

At that moment, there were two taps on the door.

'Can I come in?' an eager voice cried out.

Orson smiled. He knew this voice. He unlocked the door. 'Grandad.'

'Well, look at you!' said Grandad Frank. 'You obviously get your good looks from your mother's side of the family.'

'You're looking good too, Grandad,' said Orson. 'I like your new suit.'

Francis L. Whitlock's new suit was the perfect fit, and being back amongst the magic community seemed to have reinvigorated him.

As Orson went to close his dressing room door, another family member suddenly materialised from behind it.

'Tom!' cried Orson with delight. 'You made it.'

Uncle Tom came in quietly. 'Got the problem at work solved, thankfully. Had to really step on it to get here, but luckily the traffic lights were on my side. Just thought I'd wish you the very best of luck.'

'Ah, thanks,' said Orson.

Orson's uncle smiled. 'You look—'

'Like a magician?' said Orson.

Tom laughed. 'Exactly like a magician.'

'Something's missing,' said Orson's grandad. He took Orson's black cape down from a clothes hanger in the wardrobe and placed it over his grandson's shoulders. 'Now he looks exactly like a magician.'

Orson tied the cape and smiled at his grandfather. 'Any last words of wisdom?'

'Not from me,' replied Frank, shaking his head. 'You're a far better magician than I ever was.'

Orson had a lump in his throat.

Tom walked over to a table upon which Orson's top hat lay. Carefully, he lifted the top hat and handed it to his nephew. Orson had just placed the hat on his head, when two more taps sounded on the door.

Agatha popped her head in. 'Orson, sorry to interrupt, but you've got to do the coin toss now to see which of you perform first.'

Orson's grandad and Uncle Tom took this as their cue to leave and promptly did so, after wishing Orson all the luck in the world.

Orson lifted his white gloves from the table and pulled them on tightly. He was all set. He left his dressing room and walked along the corridor, his black cape billowing behind him.

Judging from the noise now emanating from the venue, Orson knew that the audience had finally taken their seats and that they were starting to get boisterous.

A large, shadowy form materialised at the opposite end of the corridor and Orson knew immediately who it was.

Daxton was dressed immaculately in a black suit with a red waistcoat and a white bow tie. His black hair was slicked back and his beard was neatly trimmed. He advanced quickly.

Peter, acting as the referee, called both magicians forward.

Orson made his way towards the middle of the corridor and, when he was face to face with Daxton, he stopped.

They eyeballed each other.

Orson never blinked, but Daxton was smirking.

Peter took a fifty pence coin from his jacket pocket and asked Orson to call it.

'Heads,' said Orson.

Peter flipped the coin into the air, caught it, then slapped it down on the back of his hand.

Orson and Daxton looked down at the coin, then at each other.

Daxton smiled.

Orson frowned.

CHAPTER TWENTY-SIX

The Stage is Set

Orson sat pensively in his dressing room, listening to the cheers and roars coming from the arena.

Daxton was well through his performance and, given the level of noise, he was obviously impressing the assembled crowd.

Listening to all of this was intimidating, but what else could Orson do? He removed his white gloves and took a few sips from a glass of water. He had no intention of watching Daxton. He would sit here until he was called.

In came Agatha looking every inch the magician's assistant in a beautiful white dress. 'Did you hear that?' she asked.

Orson shook his head. 'Hear what?'

'The boos!' replied Agatha cheerily. 'He's having a nightmare out there. It's turning ugly. People in the audience have started throwing eggs up at him.'

Orson had to laugh. 'I wish.'

Agatha sat down next to Orson. 'It's been a great two years, hasn't it?' she said wistfully. 'You know, whatever happens tonight, we've had a great time. All the countries we've visited. All the places we've seen. Such incredible memories and adventures!'

Orson could only nod his head in agreement.

'Ralph is backstage,' said Agatha. 'There's a fifteen-minute interval after Daxton's performance and then you're up. I'll give you a few minutes to yourself.' She got up to leave.

'Agatha,' said Orson, clasping her by the hand.

Agatha turned around.

'D'you remember the first time I walked with you to the library?' Orson asked her.

Agatha looked back at him, trying to remember. 'I think so. It was after school, right?'

'It was,' said Orson. 'You told me that you didn't believe in magic.'

'I actually do remember saying that,' replied Agatha, after a moment. 'And you told me that I might become a believer one day.'

Orson smiled at her. 'And have you?'

Agatha smiled back at him. 'I'll tell you after the performance. See you out there.' She left without another word.

The door hadn't even fully shut when it swung open again and Peter stormed in, tapping his wristwatch. 'Hurry on!' he told Orson. 'It's time you were out there. You don't want to keep your audience waiting, now, do you? Hurry on please! This way.'

Orson put on his top hat and followed Peter along the corridor.

A moment later, Peter stopped and waved his hand forward. 'Just up those stairs,' he said in a stern tone of voice.

Pulling on his gloves, Orson took a deep breath and made his way slowly forward until he came to a set of stairs. Up he went, his legs feeling like jelly and his hands starting to get clammy underneath his white gloves.

He was no stranger to these feelings, of course. Most nights before a show he'd get nervous. It was a good sign, but this performance had a lot more pressure on it.

When he reached the top of the stairs, he found himself at the side of the stage. He stood there looking around. The curtains were closed and the stagehands were hurriedly exchanging the props that Daxton had used for the ones that Orson would need.

Ralph was holding his baton in the air and was waiting patiently with the forty players of his orchestra, all of them looking primed with their various instruments and ready to go at his command.

Agatha, meanwhile, was standing on the side stage directly opposite him. Their eyes met and he smiled nervously at her. She returned the smile and nodded at him.

Orson fixed the bottom button of his waistcoat that must have come undone after he'd climbed the stairs. Tightening his white gloves, he took a deep breath and listened as a booming voice emanated from the speakers.

'Nicknamed "Orson the Great", our next magician is a sensation and is one of the hottest properties around in magic. Already touring the world to sell-out crowds, please put your hands together for Orson the Great!'

Orson took two deep breaths. This was it. The stage was set and the title of Grand Master was the bounty. The curtains parted. Throwing his arms into the air, he strode out on stage with a beaming smile.

CHAPTER TWENTY-SEVEN

The Performance

The crowd rose to their feet and this was followed by a deafening applause.

As the orchestra struck up a suitably bombastic intro in the background, Orson raised his hands and walked around the stage.

'Magic is about making people believe that the impossible is possible,' he said, loudly and clearly to the audience. 'To elicit a sense of wonder in an audience. That is my goal this evening.'

He took off his top hat and flattened it with his fist, then punched it back into shape, before showing the audience that it was empty. He then proceeded to pull a red cloth out of the hat, followed by a poster with the image of a rabbit on its front.

The crowd applauded as Orson asked for a volunteer, and selected a girl of about sixteen from the front row.

'Oh, before I forget,' announced Orson, as the girl started up the stairs, 'a big thank you must go to Daxton the Destroyer for being tonight's warm-up act.'

As laughter erupted around the auditorium, the young girl was escorted by Agatha over to Orson.

'What's your name?' asked Orson.

'Grace,' said the girl.

'That's my mother's name,' said Orson with a smile. 'She's here tonight, as well. Hi, Mum.' He handed the hat to Grace. 'Could you do me a favour, Grace, please? Could you look inside the hat and make sure that there are no secret compartments?'

Grace felt around the inside of the velvet hat and could confirm, as she showed the hat to the audience, that the interior was perfectly solid.

Orson exchanged items with Agatha. He handed her the top hat and she passed him the magic wand.

'No, you do it,' said Orson, handing Grace the magic wand.

Grace looked like she'd just been handed a stick of dynamite. 'What do you want me to do with it?'

Orson laughed. 'All you have to do is tap the hat three times.'

Grace did as she was asked and, on the third tap, a white rabbit, as cute as could be, wiggled out from inside the hat. She burst out laughing. 'That's crazy!'

Orson led the applause for Grace and the crowd gladly joined in. 'Can I keep the bunny?' she asked, cradling the rabbit.

'Unfortunately not,' replied Orson. 'But I do have something else for you.'

Agatha took the rabbit off a displeased Grace and walked off stage with it.

'These are for you,' said Orson, producing a bunch of flowers from the interior of his top hat. He handed them to her. 'I hope you have a lovely Christmas.'

'Thanks,' said Grace, blushing.

Agatha came back out with a small cardboard box and perched it on a tall, wooden stool. Then she accompanied Grace back to her seat, as Orson asked for another volunteer who might be brave enough to raise their hand and come up on stage.

Agatha had many courageous people to choose from, as hands shot up around the entire audience. Ultimately, however, she settled on a large man in the third row.

He was athletic and strong, and these were precisely the attributes that Agatha was striving to find in order to help embellish the next trick.

Up he came to the stage and told Orson that his name was Michael.

'Nice to meet you, Michael,' said Orson, shaking his hand. He nodded at the box. 'Have a look inside. Empty, isn't it?'

Michael opened the cardboard box and confirmed to the audience that it was indeed empty.

'Simple task, this,' said Orson. 'Lift the box.'

Michael cracked a smile, thinking there had to be a catch. To his surprise, he lifted the box without any difficulty.

Orson took a red handkerchief from the breast pocket of his jacket and waved it at Michael. 'This handkerchief mightn't look it, but believe me, it's very heavy. How much can you bench press?'

'About a hundred and twenty-five kilograms,' replied Michael proudly. 'On a good day.'

'Impressive,' exclaimed Orson with a smile. 'This should be easy for you.' He dropped the handkerchief into the box. Then he clasped Michael by the arm. 'Lift the box.'

Funnelling every ounce of strength he had, Michael tried in vain to lift the box off the stool, but it wouldn't budge. He tried a second time, but this attempt was even less successful than the first. The veins in his neck enlarged, his face turned red and his large biceps flexed, but he still couldn't lift the box off the stool.

Orson reached a hand inside the box and removed the handkerchief. Then he grabbed Michael by the arm again. 'I've just given you your strength back. Try again.'

Michael lifted the box with ease and chuckled. He wagged a finger at Orson. 'You're up to something!'

'I'm always up to something,' said Orson, dropping the handkerchief back into the box. 'I'm a magician. How about now?'

Michael had a baffled look on his face. Even before an attempt was made to lift the box, he was laughing uproariously.

'You see,' said Orson, 'you're overthinking it now. It's a state of mind. You're expecting the box to be heavy. It's just a handkerchief and I haven't touched your arm. You should still have your strength. You just have to believe that you can do it.'

Michael bent his knees, got down low and tried his best under the circumstances. Grimacing, he tried to heave the box up, but it didn't so much as budge. Exhausted, he gave up a lot quicker this time and gasped for breath.

Orson approached the stool and lifted the box with minimum effort.

Michael smiled. 'I knew you were up to something! I'll be awake all night trying to figure that one out.'

'Forget the box,' Orson told Michael. 'I'll give you another chance to redeem yourself.'

Agatha handed Orson a notepad and a black pen.

'I want you to think of a word,' said Orson. 'Nothing obvious like "Christmas" or your own name. A random word. Don't say it out loud, but just think it. Have you got one?'

Michael nodded. 'Yes. I've got one.'

'I want you to enlarge that word in your mind,' Orson told him. 'Make it really big, but don't tell me it yet.'

Orson stared into Michael's eyes for a long moment, then began to write on the notepad. 'That's interesting,' he said. 'I've written a word down here. I think I'm close. Please, sir, tell us what word you were thinking of?'

'Extraordinary,' said Michael.

'Well, it would be if I got this word right, wouldn't it?' said Orson. He turned the notepad around to reveal the word 'extraordinary'.

The audience applauded.

Orson ripped the page from the notepad and handed it as a souvenir to Michael, who went back to his seat smiling like a little boy.

Time tended to fly by on stage, so Orson stepped up his game.

He flung a deck of fifty-two cards into the air and found the audience member's selected card, the four of clubs, with the point of a sword.

Without pausing for breath, he then performed a card trick that resulted in a signed ace of spades vanishing from a deck and miraculously teleporting to a sealed envelope upon the table.

One after another, Orson kept the epic illusions and inconceivable effects coming, leaving the participants speechless.

Next up, he used a seemingly normal carton of milk to pour multiple drinks requested by the audience, and defied logic by transforming white handkerchiefs into doves.

After placing the doves safely into their cages, he then moved onto a levitation trick, as two stagehands wheeled out a table and Agatha reclined back on it.

Her body was covered in a large, red cloth. Orson moved a stainless steel hoop across the table to prove that no wires were being used.

Then, he stood on a platform behind the table and employed the help once more of one of the stagehands, who swiped the cloth away at his command a few moments later.

Demonstrating his extraordinary telekinetic power, Orson raised his hands upwards and Agatha began to float off the table. Then his hands stopped and Agatha hovered in mid-air at his command. She looked very peaceful, with her eyes closed and her head tilted back, as if she were in some sort of trance state.

To confound the audience even further, the table was wheeled away by both stagehands. Agatha, however, remained in her original position, floating in mid-air.

This gave Orson a moment to retrieve the steel hoop and run it across her body to emphasise the fact that no supports or wires were in operation.

The table was wheeled back on.

To complete the baffling illusion, Orson lowered Agatha back down onto the table without so much as laying a white glove on her.

The applause that followed this illusion was deafening.

Seldom did Orson pause for breath and, when he did, the boisterous crowd called out for more. With time running out, he upped the ante, focusing on illusions that he knew would leave an instant impact, while also demonstrating his range as a magician.

The orchestra played an atmospheric score as Agatha took out a chair and placed it in the middle of the stage. She sat down and Orson draped her body in a large navy-blue cloth, with her form visible underneath the covering the entire time. Grabbing the corners of the cloth with his gloved hands, Orson whisked it away to reveal an empty chair.

The effect was well received by the crowd, but it wasn't over! When Agatha reappeared in the middle of the crowd a moment later, the applause turned to cheers. In this case, the third act to the magic trick was a thing of beauty.

Poor Agatha, who was certainly earning her money tonight, had only just returned to the stage when Orson signalled for a large box to be wheeled on by attendants.

Agatha then squirmed into the box and stretched out fully.

Those of a squeamish disposition closed their eyes or looked away, just in the nick of time, as Orson took possession of a buzzsaw that was supplied to him by a stagehand and started to 'saw' his assistant in half.

It was a trick synonymous with magic over the years, but had stood the test of time very well and Orson made it his own. The many bottles of fake blood that he'd taken with him from the Centre of Excellence helped to make the trick look suitably gory.

A few minutes later, the bloodied buzzsaw was taken from Orson by a stagehand and the large box, now cut into two halves, was wheeled around the stage. The half showing Agatha's head and shoulders was wheeled to the left, while the second section with her legs and feet veered right.

When the two boxes had completed a tour of the stage and were reunited back in the middle, Agatha jumped out in one piece and waved to her adoring fans.

Joining hands, Orson and Agatha walked alongside one another towards the edge of the stage and took a bow. Then, to a thundering applause, they both levitated a few feet into the air and watched as the curtains gradually closed in front of them.

In mid-air, Agatha threw her arms around Orson's neck.

Orson smiled at her. 'Why'd you do that?'

'Thanks for everything,' replied Agatha, looking into his eyes. 'Ask me again.'

Orson's smiled widened. 'Do you believe in magic?'

'Of course I do,' said Agatha, as they descended to the stage floor behind the curtain. 'How could I not? After all that's happened since I met you.'

Orson suddenly realised that he'd got fake blood smeared all over Agatha's sparkling white dress. He apologised profusely.

Agatha hadn't even noticed. 'It doesn't matter,' she said, shaking her head. 'Nothing matters now.'

They embraced each other until the curtains opened again and, even then, it took the roar of the crowd to part them.

Magnus walked on stage and smiled at Orson, then at Agatha. 'Well done!' he said.

The orchestra finished its piece to a round of applause.

The crowd then began to cheer.

Orson suddenly realised that this was it. There was nothing more he could do. His show had been an extravaganza. And yet, for all its merits, had he done enough?

One girl seemed to think so.

'You've won, Orson!' said Agatha, whispering in his ear as she took his hand in hers. 'I just know it.'

Orson wasn't so sure. For one thing, he hadn't seen Daxton's performance, so he couldn't compare their head-to-heads. He just couldn't say for sure, one way or the other.

Daxton emerged and stood quietly in the centre of the stage with his arms by his side.

Orson tried to find his mum and dad in the crowd, but it was hard to see anyone with the stage lights shining in his eyes. He did, however, see the Grand Master's gold pin – the Holy Grail of magic – resting nearby on a red cushion, waiting for its owner to be identified.

Magnus stood in between Orson and Daxton and smiled at them both. 'Great show, gentlemen. It's a pity that there can only be one winner.'

Orson turned and saw Peter, surely one of the judges, walking up onto the stage with a white envelope clasped in his hand.

Orson's eyes widened. The result!

Magnus took the envelope off Peter and put on his reading glasses.

As Magnus unsealed the envelope, Orson continued to hold Agatha's hand in his.

From inside the envelope, Magnus removed a sheet of paper and unfolded it.

Orson felt surprisingly calm. Daxton, by contrast, looked incredibly nervous all of a sudden.

It was the first time that Orson had seen Daxton looking vulnerable. His great rival was obviously feeling the pressure, too.

Magnus held up a hand for quiet and asked the boisterous crowd to calm themselves. An expectant hush descended upon the audience.

Orson exhaled. Was he about to be crowned the winner?

Magnus fixed his glasses and smiled. 'The judges came to a unanimous decision. They based their verdict on presentation, showmanship, skill, choice of magic, technical ability and demonstration of competency.'

Covered in fake blood and all but shattered from his endeavours, Orson looked on anxiously. The tension was almost too much to bear.

There was a drum roll.

Magnus cleared his throat. 'Without further ado, the winner is—'

CHAPTER TWENTY-EIGHT

The Result

'Daxton the Destroyer.'

Orson felt everything freeze around him, as if time had suddenly stopped and only he knew about it. He felt like he'd been hypnotised and somehow, in his trance state, he'd heard the wrong name being declared as the winner.

He'd lost! His hopes and dreams were shattered.

The announcement of Daxton as the winner sparked wild celebrations. Everyone in the audience were up on their feet, banging walls and cheering the victor's name.

Orson could hear very little from then on. The shock took over. Agatha was still holding his hand, but numerous people had jumped up on stage. They were Daxton's supporters, clearly, and they were simply delirious looking.

Even Peter, the stuffy-looking judge, who had been quite rude to him earlier, was now clapping and laughing hysterically. Pure elation was etched on his face.

Orson turned red. Why was Peter so happy? Peter hadn't so much as raised a smile since Orson had met him, but now here he was laughing uproariously. As a judge, wasn't he supposed to remain neutral? Was Peter a supporter of Daxton?

Orson fought the impulse to remove the bottle of fake blood from his jacket pocket and throw it all over Peter's sparkling white suit. He was giving this evil thought serious consideration, when Agatha turned him around to face her.

'Let's get out of here!' she said.

Orson was looking around at all the equipment and machinery behind the stage that had been taken from the Centre of Excellence.

Agatha read between the lines. 'The van will take all the equipment back to your house.'

Orson nodded. 'I'll go get changed.' There were so many people surrounding Daxton that Orson couldn't even see where the victorious magician was. At least that was a bit of positive news. He didn't want to see Daxton ever again.

Orson and Agatha fought their way through the celebrations. They left the stage, one behind the other, Orson avoiding eye contact with anyone who came his way.

He was showered, changed and ready to go within fifteen minutes. On the verge of tears, he left his dressing room and closed the door behind him.

Given the fact that he was still deflated, it was a small mercy that the corridor was quiet. He walked further along the corridor and knocked on Agatha's dressing room door.

There was no reply, so he went towards the exit at the end of the corridor. Out of the corner of his eye, he saw Agatha handing over a brown envelope stacked full of money to Ralph.

'It's all there, isn't it?' said Ralph, opening the envelope and peeping in. 'I don't have time to count it.'

Orson sighed when he spotted Ralph pinching a few fifty pound notes from the envelope. Then, in a sleight of hand that any magician would be proud of, the conductor slipped the notes surreptitiously into the back pocket of his trousers.

'You didn't see that!' exclaimed Ralph, waving the brown envelope in the air and grinning at Orson. 'Send me next year's schedule. Merry Christmas, Orson.'

Orson waved back.

Agatha walked over to Orson, shaking her head. 'Right, let's go. My dad is waiting for me. Your mum and dad are outside, too.'

Orson knew he had to face everyone again at some point, so he nodded and followed sheepishly behind Agatha. They left the hotel through the back door and, when he got outside, Orson saw his entire family waiting for him in the car park.

'You did great tonight, Orson,' said Agatha, taking his hands in hers. 'You should be very proud of yourself. Merry Christmas!'

'Merry Christmas to you too, Agatha,' replied Orson, trying to smile.

Their hands finally parted. Orson watched Agatha walk across the car park until she was out of sight.

If his family were disappointed, they certainly weren't showing it. Orson had never seen them looking happier. His dad was sharing a joke with Uncle Tom, and his grandad was talking jovially with his mum and grandma.

'Hi,' said Orson, looking down at his shoes.

A rapturous round of applause went up.

'Here's the man of the moment,' said his grandad, clapping furiously.

Orson's mum and dad walked over and threw their arms around him.

'What an incredible performance,' said Martin Whitlock, his eyes bright with pride. 'All those hours practising in the Centre of Excellence certainly paid off.'

Tom laughed. 'You were incredible, Orson. Simply incredible. A flawless performance. Very well done.'

His family were all talking over each other, but their sentiments were similar – they all thought he'd performed to a very high standard.

The consensus was that his performance had been a potent mixture of showmanship, sleight of hand, misdirection and mentalism. All these elements, coupled with his infectious personality, made for great entertainment.

Orson's mum was shaking her head. 'We were sure you'd won.'

'But I didn't win,' said Orson tearfully.

Martin Whitlock was smiling. 'All is not lost,' he said mysteriously. 'In magic, things aren't always what they seem. You know that.'

Orson narrowed his eyes. 'What d'you mean, Dad?'

'We'll talk more about it when we get home,' replied his dad.

Orson hopped into the family car, wondering what his dad could possibly mean. Uncle Tom was chauffeuring Orson's grandparents in his car and, before they went their separate ways, they all agreed to rendezvous back at the house.

The cars drove off.

Sitting in the back seat of the car, Orson looked out his window ruefully. He just had one question for his dad. 'What happens now, Dad?'

'We go home, Orson,' said his dad. 'We go home.'

Orson looked out at the Christmas trees in the windows of the passing houses. Going home sounded like the greatest plan he'd ever heard.

Several minutes later, the car drove through the gates of the house and pulled up in the drive. Unbuckling his seatbelt, Orson gazed at the Christmas tree shining in the conservatory. He felt better already. He was home.

When he got inside, the kitchen table was set for seven people. Seven! He did a quick headcount. Just as he had thought. There were six people, including himself.

Maybe Uncle Brian was calling around. Or perhaps his auntie from the parish of Tydavnet in County Monaghan had flown over for Christmas. That was an exciting thought. His Irish relatives were such lovely people. The fact that they always brought over great presents was a bonus.

Orson was famished and he couldn't remember a time when he had looked forward to the traditional Christmas Eve dinner more. Vegetable soup was the starter and Orson was assigned the task of bringing it to the boil.

As he stirred the large pot on the stove, his mind kept puzzling over what had gone wrong earlier. Should he have started with the levitation act first, rather than at the end? Was his performance a little light on card tricks? Were the judges expecting to see more cardistry? He sensed he might never get any answers to these questions.

By the time the soup had boiled, Orson's grandfather had already consumed two glasses of brandy, and was well into his third when he began to tell jokes around the table.

Orson took a teaspoon from the cutlery drawer and tasted the simmering soup. It was delicious, but he could take no credit. He was about to compliment his mum's wondrous cooking, when his grandad called out to him.

'Come on, Orson, my dear boy. Hurry on there!'

Orson jumped.

Grandad Frank thumbed the table with his soup spoon. 'Are you going to share the soup, or eat it all yourself?!'

Orson laughed as his mum rolled her eyes at him.

Orson seasoned the soup with salt and chopped basil. Then he spooned the soup into deep bowls and carried them over, two at a time, to the table.

Orson's grandad garnished his soup with a few drops of cream, before slurping a spoonful. He sighed with contentment. 'Merry Christmas, everyone,' he said.

Orson sat down last of all and took his soup. It was delicious! All in all, there were several different ingredients in the mix – carrots, courgette, parsnips, potatoes, tomatoes, peas, pumpkin and a healthy serving of cream, too.

'The soup's delicious, Grace,' remarked Uncle Tom, buttering his crusty bread roll.

Grandma Alice, halfway through her soup already, seconded that sentiment.

On such a cold night, everyone remarked how cosy and warm the kitchen was. The oven was on, roasting the turkey, and this added even more warmth to the room.

By the time Orson had finished his soup, he did feel a whole lot better. His defeat to Daxton hadn't been mentioned once. It would only cast a dark cloud over the evening. He knew nobody wanted to speak about it. There was a time and a place and this wasn't it.

What was strange, however, was the one empty chair opposite him at the table. The place had been set and a plate was already out for the main course.

By now, Grandad Frank had nearly finished his third double brandy. 'I remember my reveal like it was yesterday. Where do the years go?'

'Your reveal?' asked Orson, narrowing his eyes. 'What does that mean, Grandad?'

Orson's dad placed his soup spoon down. 'That's what I want to talk to you about, Orson. I've something to tell you.'

The doorbell chimed suddenly. Orson looked around the kitchen and saw some very strange sights indeed. His mum and dad were laughing, while his grandparents were nudging each other and smiling.

At least he had an ally in Uncle Tom, who looked every bit as bemused by the sudden eruption of laughter at the dinner table.

Orson shook his head. Was he missing something? A visitor to the house on Christmas Eve wasn't out of the ordinary. If anything, it was customary for neighbours to exchange gifts.

Usually, around this time on Christmas Eve, Orson would pop over to the Johnstons, followed by the Morgans to deliver a tin of biscuits, a box of chocolates, and sometimes a bottle of wine, too.

Given the events of the day, he hadn't gotten around to doing this yet, so one of the neighbours had obviously decided to deliver the presents themselves.

Orson's dad smiled at him. 'You get that, Orson,' he told him.

It suddenly occurred to Orson what was going on. The spare place at the table was set for Agatha! His assistant had been invited over for dinner. Of course she had. The thought of seeing Agatha again sent his heart racing.

He got up and hugged his dad. 'Thanks, Dad.' Then he ran out of the kitchen and along the corridor. The bell chimed again and Orson scrambled to unlock the door.

In great haste, he swung the door open with a beaming smile. However, owing to the thick fog, it was impossible to see who was standing in the shadows.

Finally, a figure stepped into the moonlight. It wasn't Agatha.

Orson could scarcely believe his own eyes. What was going on?

It was Daxton.

Orson froze and his face turned as pale as the moon in the sky.

Daxton advanced forward. 'We need to talk.'

CHAPTER TWENTY-NINE

The Revelation

If Orson could've formed a sentence, he would've done it by now. He just stood there in shock, holding the door open.

'Can I come in?' asked Daxton. His voice was friendly and warm.

'Of course you can,' said a welcoming voice.

Orson wasn't sure if he had spoken these words. He didn't think he had. However, as he was in a state of complete shock, he wasn't sure of anything anymore.

As it turned out, he hadn't spoken. His dad was standing behind him.

'Come in, Daxton,' said Martin Whitlock. 'You're very welcome.'

In Daxton came, wiping his shoes on the doormat before walking any further.

Orson's eyes followed him.

Martin Whitlock greeted Daxton with the secret handshake that Orson had seen a few times by now. Then they hugged.

'Merry Christmas, Marty,' said Daxton.

'Merry Christmas to you too, Daxton,' said Orson's dad. 'Right this way.'

Daxton was dressed suavely in a grey, two-piece suit and white shirt. 'Something smells good,' he said. 'Sorry I'm late.'

Orson felt like his hand was glued to the doorframe.

'Orson, shut the door,' said his dad with a shiver. 'It's freezing.'

Orson shut the door and stood there in a daze. Was he having a nightmare? Was this really happening, or was it some sort of prank? Was it Uncle Brian in disguise, wearing one of those realistic masks from the Centre of Excellence?

The nightmare, the prank and Uncle Brian in disguise – any one of these explanations would've made much more sense to Orson than Daxton standing in his house.

Daxton went into the kitchen and shook everybody's hand.

Orson, once again, noted the secret handshake that was conducted between Daxton and his grandad.

'Daxton, can I offer you a brandy?' asked Grandad Frank, reaching for the bottle.

Daxton shook his head. 'Not for me thanks, Francis. I've the car.'

Orson somehow managed to sit back down on his chair and stared blankly ahead.

Daxton sat down and smiled. 'What a night, huh?'

Not having a clue about what was going on, Orson looked at his dad for some answers.

His dad shrugged. 'We've some explaining to do, haven't we?'

Orson looked over at his mum, who was stirring the saucepan of gravy on the stove. She was carrying on as if dinner was the single most important thing happening in the kitchen right now.

Orson felt like shouting 'What is going on?!' at the top of his voice, but he didn't get the chance.

Daxton removed the Grand Master's pin from his jacket.

'If you've come to gloat,' said Orson, pointing to the door, 'you can leave right now.'

Daxton threw the pin in the bin next to him.

Orson stood up, appalled.

'There is *no* Grand Master's pin, Orson,' said Daxton. 'Because there is no Grand Master. There is no split in the Society of Magicians. We're all members and friends.'

Orson looked at his dad for confirmation.

His dad gave a gentle nod.

'But the book I got in the library,' said Orson. 'It said that there *was* a split in the Society of Magicians.'

Daxton nodded. 'We published the book ourselves and left it in the library for you to find. Every member we recruit reads the same book, so we can plant the split narrative into their minds.'

Orson sat back down and looked once more at his dad, who nodded.

Daxton smiled. 'You might remember that I met you in the library the day you chose that book. A little earlier, I'd left the book sitting out slightly. It was done on purpose. We wanted you to read it.'

'We had to set up the story, Orson,' said his dad. 'That's also why I told you that this man...' he added, pointing to Daxton, '...was dangerous, and that he'd do anything to become Grand Master. By creating a rival, it pushed you and kept you focused.'

Francis L. Whitlock topped up his brandy. 'It was the motivation you needed, Orson. That's why we created a story. It gave you challenges to overcome, and boy did it work. Look at the heights you've scaled in such a short space of time.'

'Grandad is right,' said Martin Whitlock. 'The experience you received was priceless. Be honest – if we hadn't created a narrative around the Society of Magicians and given you a rival to pit yourself against, would you have persevered as much as you have?'

'Probably not,' replied Orson.

Orson's grandad smiled at him. 'We gave you the motivation that you needed to succeed. It was completely up to you whether you showed the necessary tenacity and resilience.'

Orson was starting to come around to this elaborate plot. 'So, that's why the three of you are in the photograph in the Centre of Excellence?'

Daxton laughed. 'That was taken on the day of my reveal. I went through the exact same experience that you did, but I was older than you, Orson. You're now the youngest ever member to be inducted into the Society of Magicians. You really are a special talent.'

'Did you know about all this, Tom?' asked Orson, turning to his uncle.

Tom, who'd sat quietly sipping his white wine and listening to the conversation, started to squirm in his seat. 'Well, I knew you weren't going to the dentist!' he admitted. 'And I knew it had something to do with magic.'

'Oh, okay,' said Orson.

Tom sighed. 'I'm also not an accountant anymore. I sell insurance. I spend a lot of my time now on the road. I'm a terrible liar, so I didn't want to talk too much about it on the train to Edinburgh.'

'Speaking of Edinburgh,' said Orson. 'There were two magicians at my fake inauguration in Edinburgh.' He stopped and glanced over at his dad. 'That was fake, right?'

Orson's dad smiled and nodded. 'It was a set-up, yes. Good day out, though?'

'I loved Edinburgh,' replied Orson, turning to Daxton as he said this. 'But when I was there, I met two magicians and they told me that you were responsible for other members in the Society of Magicians going missing.'

'Oh, that was Harry and John-Paul,' explained Daxton. 'No, they were told to say that. As was Magnus. All three of them quite enjoy casting aspersions on my character.'

'And the boy you were shouting at backstage?'

Daxton nodded. 'My nephew, Raymond. He's a budding actor. He joined the local dramatics society a few years ago. He was acting.'

Orson made a face. 'Did you know I was watching?'

'Yes,' said Daxton, 'we both knew you were watching.'

Martin Whitlock interjected. 'A small percentage of our members do believe that a split has occurred in the Society of Magicians, but they really are in the minority. We feel it helps to keep the pretence up.'

Daxton shook his head. 'Poor Albert Matthews doesn't know. Isn't that right, Martin?'

'No, Albert doesn't know,' replied Orson's dad. 'We need to keep a certain number of members out of the loop to believably set up recruits. My friend Albert, for example, will eventually be told the truth, and then somebody else will take his place and so on.'

'So I was recruited?' asked Orson.

'Yes, you were,' replied his dad. 'We need to improve our numbers. One of the goals of the Society of Magicians is to recruit more members. A whole new generation of magicians.'

Orson's grandad said, 'We want magic to return to its heyday of the 1920s and 1930s.'

'The golden age of magic,' said Orson.

Grandad Frank chuckled. 'I remember magic in the 1920s and the 1930s very well. Some amazing magicians at the height of their powers.' He sipped his brandy.

'I can imagine,' said Orson.

'But the golden age spanned long before the 1920s and 1930s,' said Grandad Frank. 'Magic was huge at the end of the nineteenth century as well. The 1880s and 1890s.'

Orson smiled to himself.

'No, Orson,' said his grandad. 'I don't quite remember those two decades.'

Orson cracked another smile and threw his hands up. 'I didn't say anything.'

'You didn't have to,' exclaimed his grandad. 'Like all good magicians, I read your mind.'

Orson laughed.

'But what a time it was,' resumed Frank. 'So today, members of the Society of Magicians go out into the world and try to introduce magic to people to restore our great art form back to its former glories. It's very admirable.'

'Magic is one of the oldest performing arts in the world,' said Daxton. 'We're all magicians, because we were inspired by the careers of the performers who came before us. We stand on the shoulders of giants.'

'A metaphor by Isaac Newton, I believe,' said Grandad Frank, raising his glass of brandy. 'Well said, Daxton! Well said!'

'It's our duty to try to keep our craft alive,' said Martin Whitlock.

Daxton nodded. 'All it takes is one good trick for a child to fall in love with magic. Just one!'

'Can we eat now?' said Orson's grandmother, sitting patiently with her arms folded and looking glumly at the empty plate on the table before her.

Everybody laughed, including Orson's mum, who by now had taken the turkey out of the oven and had set it down on the countertop next to the sink.

Daxton sighed. 'Congratulations, Orson. You passed every single obstacle we put in your way. I've a son about your age and I'm just starting to get him into magic. He's a big fan of yours. I'd love you to meet him.'

'I'd love to,' said Orson. 'What's his name?'

'Adam,' said Daxton.

'Okay,' said Grace Whitlock, 'enough magic talk. I need help. Fetch the cranberry sauce for me, Martin, please.'

Orson's dad got up quickly. 'Of course, dear.'

'So that's everything out in the open,' said Orson's grandfather. 'Another recruit.'

Daxton smiled and sat back in his chair, looking relieved to finally have the whole ordeal over with. 'I'm starving.'

The food was gradually placed on the table and it didn't last long. Everybody helped themselves. There was plenty to go around, but Orson, even when he was eating, couldn't stop staring at Daxton. It was very surreal to be sitting opposite a man whom he thought, just a few hours ago, was his greatest rival.

'You're the greatest magician I've ever seen,' said Orson admiringly.

Daxton smiled graciously. 'Thanks,' he replied, sipping his tea. 'I've worked very hard to become so. I've spent many years refining my skills.' He leant across the table and pointed his fork at Orson. 'You're not so bad yourself.'

Orson placed his knife and fork down. 'So you were pretending to be happy tonight?'

'What was that?' said Daxton, pouring gravy over his mashed potatoes.

'You know, when the result was called out,' said Orson, eating a Brussel sprout.

Daxton tucked into his dinner. 'Yeah. What about it?'

'You looked so happy,' said Orson. 'Were you acting when the result was called out?'

Orson's dad was shaking his head.

'You must be joking?!' replied Daxton, chewing. 'I was delighted! I've never lost to a recruit before and, for the first time ever, members had placed bets against me winning.'

Orson was flattered. 'Really?'

Daxton nodded. 'We're talking high stake bets here, Orson. I didn't want to lose to you. Some magicians in the society thought that you were going to beat me. That has never happened. My pride was at stake.'

Orson smiled.

'So, I'm sorry, Orson,' continued Daxton. 'But the celebrations were genuine. I'm a proud man. I wanted to win more than anything, and a lot of the members were rooting for me as well!'

'Let me guess,' said Orson. 'The man in the white suit had money on you to win.'

Daxton burst out laughing. 'Who, Peter? Erm, yes, I believe he had.' He brought his index finger and thumb together. 'You were this close to beating me, Orson. I saw the judges' scorecard. I met my match this evening. It was so close.'

This made Orson feel an awful lot better about himself. 'Well, I want a rematch in the new year.'

'Done!' said Daxton, laughing. 'A 1973 rematch. That should draw the crowds in.'

'Right,' said Grace Whitlock with a deep sigh. 'Enough magic for one night.'

Orson let out a laugh. 'Okay, Mum. You're right.'

Magic was put to one side. Over the desserts of sherry trifle and plum pudding with hot custard, they sat around the table talking about anything other than card tricks, levitations, mentalism and showmanship.

Orson was relieved to finally be able to discuss other topics, even if one of those revolved around his school timetable for this year. He also discovered that his grandparents were celebrating their fiftieth wedding anniversary next year.

'What's your secret?' asked Daxton.

Alice Whitlock laughed. 'Avoiding each other for forty-five of them.'

'Fourteen years,' said Daxton, when Orson's grandmother asked him how long he and his lovely wife Sarah had been married.

The Christmas crackers were snapped open.

Orson went up against Daxton and won. A novelty gift of a miniature deck of cards flew out onto the table.

As Orson placed the red-coloured paper crown on his head, his dad made a wisecrack comment about the fact that his son had, at last, beaten Daxton at something that day.

Grace Whitlock admonished her husband, but Orson burst out laughing.

Daxton lifted the miniature deck of cards from between the salt and pepper shakers. 'It just had to be a deck of cards,' he said, handing them to Orson. 'You keep them.'

'I'll put them in the Centre of Excellence,' said Orson, already generating ideas in his head on how best to use the miniature cards for the embellishment of a trick.

Orson politely refused the pudding and, instead, took a second helping of the trifle.

'Do you not like pudding, Orson?' asked his grandmother, eating her own portion with relish.

'No, Grandma, or Christmas cake,' said Orson. 'You take my slice.'

His grandma smiled at him. 'I might just do that, Orson. Thank you.'

The chocolate box was torn open and the contents were spread out like treasures upon the table.

After Daxton had chosen a couple of the hazelnut chocolates, he stood up and tapped his wristwatch. 'I better make my way home,' he announced.

'It's Christmas Eve, after all, and I've been away from home all day. My family are waiting for me.'

Martin Whitlock stood up and shook Daxton's hand. There were no secret variations this time, just a firm handshake.

Daxton turned to Orson's mum. 'Thank you, Grace, for your hospitality. Goodnight Francis, Alice and Tom. A Merry Christmas to you all.'

'Merry Christmas!' said everyone at the table in unison.

Orson followed Daxton out of the kitchen and along the corridor.

Daxton let himself out the front door. He stood on the doorstep and turned around to face Orson. 'This must've been a very strange experience for you, Orson?'

Orson nodded. 'It was.'

'I have something for you,' said Daxton.

Orson smiled. 'Do you?'

'Hold out your hand,' said Daxton, who then took a gold pin from the inner pocket of his jacket. 'You should have this.'

'I thought you threw the pin in the bin?' cried Orson, feigning surprise as he held out his hand.

Daxton smiled. 'No, you didn't. It was the best-looking fake pin I could get my hands on at short notice.' He placed the pin in the palm of Orson's outstretched hand. 'If there really was such a thing as a Grand Master, then you undoubtedly would be it!'

Orson had a lump in his throat.

Daxton gave Orson an admiring look, before turning towards his black Rolls-Royce that was parked outside the gates. 'Goodnight, Orson.'

Orson called out as the older magician walked away. 'Daxton!'

Daxton turned around.

Orson was bright-eyed. 'Would you like to call around some evening to see the Centre of Excellence? We could discuss the future of magic. And maybe we could go over some routine ideas in the theatre.'

Daxton smiled. 'I would like that.' He walked back over to Orson and held out his hand.

Orson shook Daxton's hand warmly.

'Merry Christmas, "Orson the Great",' said Daxton with a smile.

Orson watched Daxton J. Auger walk down the drive in admiration. When Daxton had driven away in his Rolls-Royce, Orson shivered. It was freezing, but what a beautiful Christmas Eve night it was.

A hard frost lay on the ground, the stars were glittering in the sky and there wasn't a sound to be heard. What an amazing Christmas Eve it had been. It had everything. Tension, great joy, terrible lows and, finally, a surprise twist he'd never seen coming.

He looked down at the gold pin in his hand and read the inscription under the silvery moonlight. 'I believe in magic,' he said in a low voice.

And indeed he did!

He smiled and closed the front door.

CHAPTER THIRTY

Christmas Day, 1972

Any other Christmas morning, Orson would've been the first member of the household up and dressed. However, the exertions of the previous day had taken their toll.

He was still sound asleep at eight forty-five when his grandfather knocked nine times on his bedroom door. Yes! Nine times!

Seeing this wasn't enough to rouse his grandson, Francis L. Whitlock began to sing a Christmas song at the top of his voice. Great song, terrible rendition.

Orson threw off his blankets and got up. Anything to stop his grandad from finishing the song! Besides, the day was full of promise.

After a quick shower, he got dressed in a grey suit and ran downstairs to open his presents. However, his mum told him that they would have to wait until after mass.

He reluctantly agreed, and opened the last window of the advent calendar hanging on the hallway wall on his way into the kitchen.

He got himself a glass of orange juice and a bowl of cereal. Then, after brushing his teeth, he was the first one in the car.

Orson's dad locked up the house and did the driving. Orson's mum sat in the passenger seat, while Orson was in the back with his grandparents either side of him.

They were in church in good time and took their places in the side aisle, from where Orson could see Agatha rehearsing with the choir up in the gallery.

They locked eyes and Agatha tried unsuccessfully to smother her laughter. The choirmistress narrowed her eyes, wondering what was suddenly so funny.

Orson held himself together much better. He simply smiled up at Agatha. He wasn't even sure why she was laughing.

Perhaps it was the fact that they'd been through so much together and an unbreakable bond was there. Or maybe she was just happy to see him. She wore a winter dress and her shiny black hair was tied back. Even at a distance, Orson thought she had a new pair of glasses, too.

People of all ages came in gradually and there was an air of excitement that Orson knew was only possible on Christmas morning.

By the time mass had started, the church was packed and Orson could see Agatha playing the organ as the choir gave an assured rendition of 'Joy to the World'.

Throughout the mass, Orson knelt and stood at the appropriate times. He listened attentively to the readings, the hymns, the Responsorial Psalm and the Gospel of Luke which told the story of Jesus Christ's birth.

Orson was cast as Joseph in the school nativity play a couple of years ago and knew this story very well. He shook every single person's hand in his row in an offering of peace and went up for communion when the time to do so arrived.

After the final blessing, he looked over at his parents, his grandparents and Uncle Tom in the opposite aisle. He really couldn't think of another place in the entire world he'd rather be.

And, when 'Hark the Herald Angels Sing' was belted out by more or less every soul crammed inside the church, he could feel the hairs on the back of his neck standing up.

The trumpet player brought the hymn to its mighty conclusion, and the Whitlocks stayed long after the mass had ended to mingle with their friends and neighbours.

Orson joined his mum and a few more people before the crib of Bethlehem, and he used the time to say a prayer for every member of his family.

Then he spun around and smiled up at Agatha in the gallery when most of the congregation had moved their discussions outside into the frost and snow.

'Is that your boyfriend down there?' the choirmistress asked Agatha.

Agatha smiled down at Orson. 'His name is Orson and, yes, he is my boyfriend.' She ran down the stairs in under ten seconds and walked with Orson towards the side exit.

'Exquisite-looking dress,' said Orson.

Agatha turned scarlet, matching the colour of her dress. 'Ah, thanks. It's new. So, did you get over your disappointment?'

Orson suddenly realised that Agatha knew absolutely nothing about the elaborate set-up that had been played on him. How could he even start to explain it? He still didn't quite understand it all himself yet.

'I've something *big* to tell you,' said Orson. 'It's about last night, but it's a long story.'

Agatha grimaced. 'My mum's waiting for me. Will you tell me it later?'

'Yeah,' said Orson. 'Can we hang out sometime? You know, when we're not practising magic or touring around Europe, or when we're in school.'

'Or heading to the library?' said Agatha.

Orson nodded. 'Yeah, like some other time?'

Agatha gave him a bashful look. 'That would be great!'

'What day is it?' asked Orson.

Agatha smiled. 'Christmas Day!'

'No,' said Orson with a giggle. 'What actual day is it?'

'I always forget what day of the week it is at Christmas, too,' said Agatha. 'It's Monday.'

'So, maybe Wednesday I can call around?' asked Orson. 'We could go to the cinema maybe?'

'Sounds good,' said Agatha. 'Merry Christmas, Orson! Have a great day with your family.'

'Merry Christmas, Agatha,' replied Orson, who watched Agatha closely as she walked down the lane and got into her mother's car.

And then, suddenly, she jumped back out again and came running towards him. She pulled Orson in for a lingering hug. 'Call at my house on Wednesday!' she whispered in his ear.

'I will,' promised Orson.

Agatha smiled and ran back towards her car. This time, her mother drove off, but Orson continued to wave, and Agatha smiled back at him through her window until the car was out of sight.

Orson and his family were home in five minutes and the presents were opened thereafter. Orson was delighted with his gifts – a jacket from Uncle

Tom, a pair of slippers from his mum, three new shirts of varying colours from his grandparents, and a quiz book from his dad.

Relatives were phoned and Orson spoke to his grandparents in Ireland. Grandad and Grandma McCormack informed Orson that they were travelling over to England in a few days to visit and that they were bringing a big bag of presents with them.

A little later, Orson helped set the table in preparation for dinner, while his dad did his customary rounds of the neighbouring houses to wish everyone a Merry Christmas.

Orson went into the living room, turned on the television and, before too long, he'd fallen asleep on the couch. When he awoke one hour later, he followed the sound of voices into the kitchen and discovered that his dad had returned.

Not long after, his uncle arrived and they all sat down for Christmas dinner. The leftover food from last night was reheated in the oven.

The trifle was running out, but an apple pie that Orson's mum produced from the fridge more than made up for this troubling development.

After the washing-up was done, they retired to the living room with a pot of hot tea and sat lazily before the cosy fire with the radio playing softly in the background.

Over the next hour, they used the quiz book to test their general knowledge. Orson paired up with his dad, while his mum was in a team of three with her in-laws.

'What country is Strasbourg in?' asked Martin Whitlock, kicking off round one.

Orson's grandma laughed and lifted her team's answer sheet from the table. 'I've been there.' After scribbling down 'France', she opened a box of chocolates and passed them around.

Whispering to one another, Orson and his dad came to a mutual decision that the answer was 'France', although they had both considered Germany at one stage.

There were seven rounds with ten questions each and categories included arts and culture, geography, history, sports, movies, music and general knowledge.

Orson did very well on the sporting questions, but less so on history and geography, but it was fun to try to guess the correct answers. His grandma, however, was the star of the entire quiz, having a solid knowledge of nearly every category, except sports, which she openly admitted she had no interest in.

The answer sheets were collected and the results verified. Despite being outnumbered, Orson and his dad managed to shade a close contest.

Francis L. Whitlock's cheating allegations against his son and grandson were unfounded and, in any case, denied by both parties, but the claims provided a lot of laughs.

'"It's A Wonderful Life" is on TV soon,' said Alice Whitlock, getting up to switch on the television, before pushing her armchair closer to the hearth.

Orson was wedged in between his mum and dad on the couch. Positioning himself in the armchair, Orson's grandad got himself comfortable and was asleep within five minutes with the newspaper, turned to the television listings, resting upon his lap.

Meanwhile, Orson's grandma's full attention was on the television and on what she described as her favourite film.

Orson hugged his mum, then his dad.

'What was that for?' asked his mum, squeezing her son's hand a little tighter.

Orson shrugged. 'I'm just glad you're both here this Christmas, that's all.'

Orson's dad smiled across at him. 'We are, too.'

During the film, Orson got up and helped himself to a few chocolates that were in a silver tray on the coffee table. He was about to leave the room, when he heard a song playing.

The volume on the radio had been turned up and his parents were now dancing and laughing. This stopped Orson in his tracks. He didn't think he had ever seen his parents looking so happy.

Orson's grandfather had woken up and was now watching his son and daughter-in-law closely. He smiled over at Orson. Then, rolling back the years, he sprang up, stretched his legs, and tried to entice his good wife up from her seat to join the spontaneous dance.

'It's Christmas Day!' cried Orson's grandad, trying to drag his wife onto the makeshift dancefloor. 'Alice, my darling, Christmas Day! Come on!'

After some consideration, Alice Whitlock thanked her husband for asking, but declined the kind offer. At least for the time being. She was far too busy hitting the side of the television set, trying to resolve the interference that had suddenly broken out on the screen.

Orson was pulled onto the dancefloor instead by his grandfather, and they swung each other around until they were both dizzy and had to sit down.

As Orson's grandad settled back into his armchair in a joyous haze, Orson found himself back on his feet again in no time as his mum linked arms with him and twirled him around. He was soon dancing, arm in arm, with both his mum and his dad, as they jived into the kitchen and back out again.

'What's gotten into all of you?' cried Alice Whitlock, trying to smother her laughter.

Eventually, when the music had stopped, they all sat down, breathless.

Orson was crying with laughter when he got back up and went towards the door of the living room. If he didn't take this course of action, he felt that he might collapse from laughter at any moment.

'Where are you going, Orson?' panted his grandad. 'The party's just starting.'

His grandmother turned around in her armchair. 'Don't miss the ending of the film, Orson. It's the best part. Clarence gets his wings.' She took hold of his hand. 'I thought you'd save me a dance, too.'

'I have saved you a dance, Grandma,' said Orson, patting her hand.

'Then stay,' pleaded his grandma.

'Listen to your grandmother,' said his dad. 'Stay Orson!'

'Don't be leaving so soon,' said his mum, laughing. 'Come back, Orson.'

I'll be back in a minute!' said Orson, giving his grandmother a hug on his way to the door. He smiled back at his family. All eyes were on him. 'I promise.'

With a huge smile on his face, he left the living room, walked briskly along the corridor and entered his father's workshop. The clocks were ticking nosily as he flicked on the lights.

Taking a moment, he looked around the workshop. A wonderful array of clocks adorned the walls of the room. His father was truly a master in more ways than one.

The bookshelf, once considered a closely guarded secret within the Whitlock household, was wide open. He made his way along the passageway, up the stairs, across the balcony and down the ladder into the Centre of Excellence.

The Centre of Excellence held a special place in his heart. He walked around slowly, taking everything in. He found a pair of white gloves in a drawer and slipped them on, as if he were a surgeon about to perform an operation.

Running his gloved hand across the glass cabinets and magical equipment, Orson entered the theatre and walked slowly down the middle aisle.

He jumped up on stage.

Whether he was performing to an empty theatre or to ten thousand adoring fans, it didn't seem to matter. The adrenaline rush was invariably the same.

He went to the centre of the stage and stood underneath the spotlight. There was nothing more left to do but thank his wonderful audience, who had come along on this once-in-a-lifetime adventure with him.

Throwing his hands theatrically into the air, he took a bow. 'You've been an incredible audience. Thank you. Bye for now!'

The red curtains closed.

Made in the USA
Columbia, SC
28 June 2023

19486547R00117